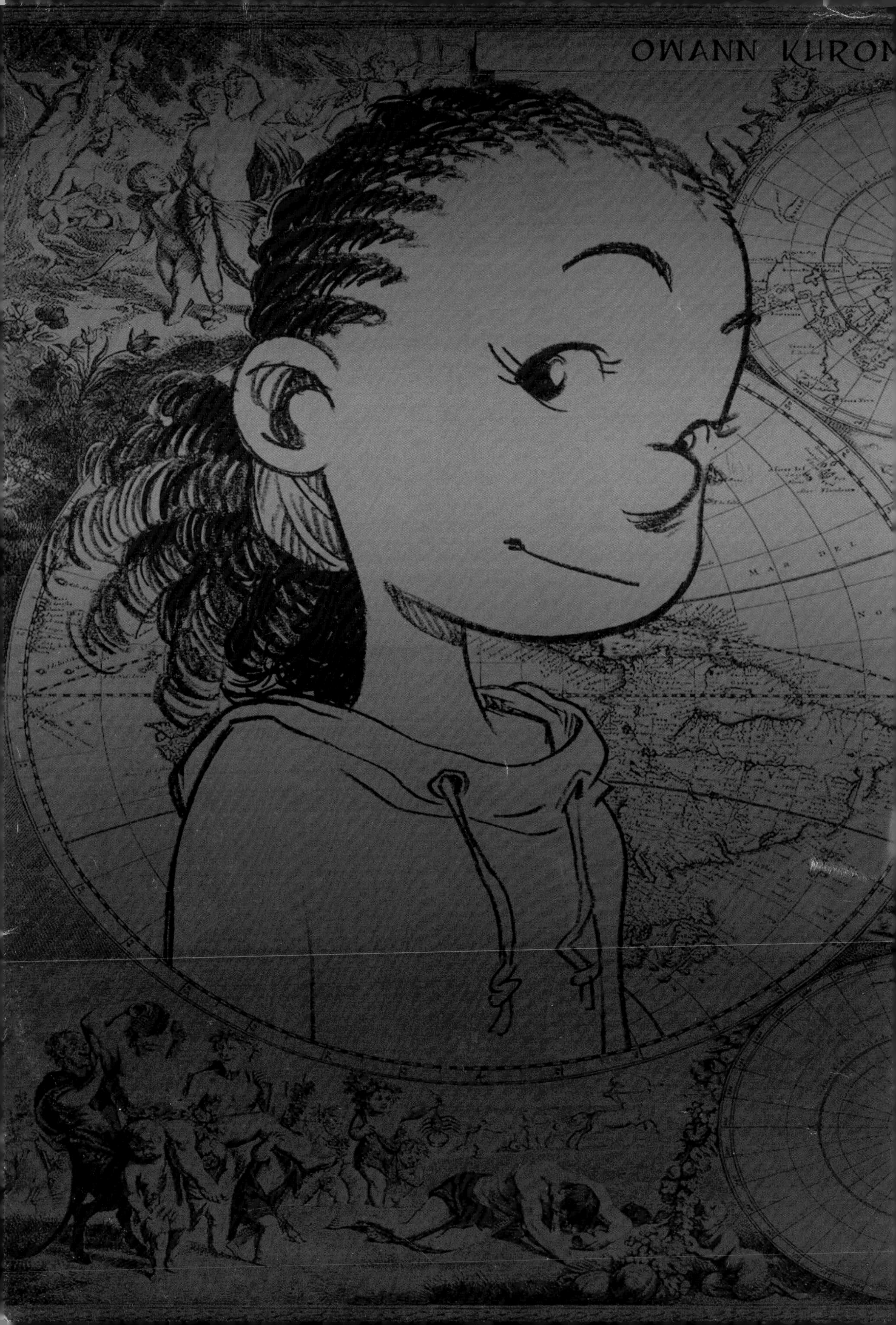
OWANN KURON

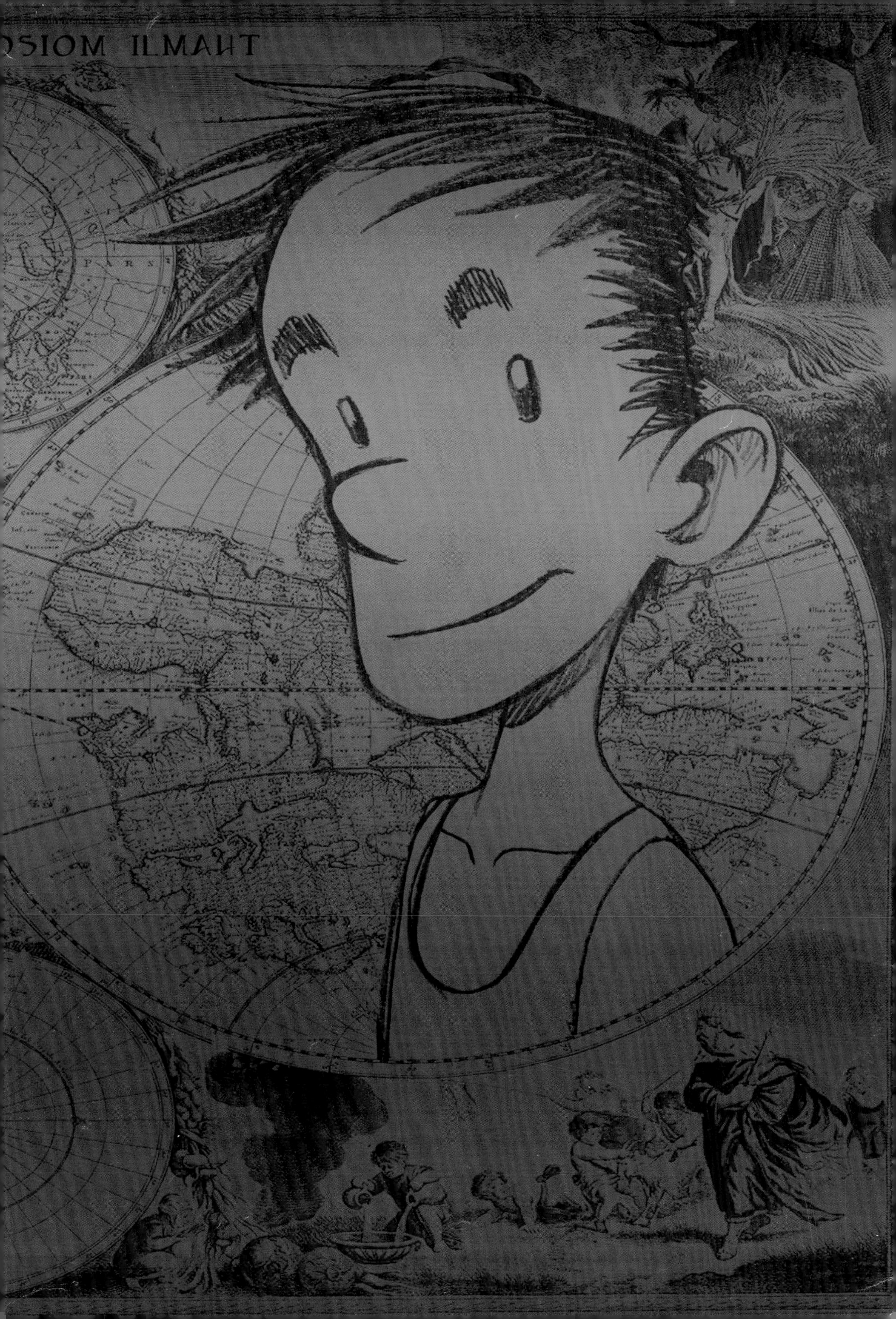

the ElseWhere CHRONICLES

BOOK FOUR
THE CALLING

ART
BANNISTER

STORY
NYKKO

COLORS
JAFFRÉ

GRAPHIC UNIVERSE™ · MINNEAPOLIS · NEW YORK

A huge thANk you to Flo foR his
iNdispeNsAble dAily suppoRt
BRAvo to LauReNce, Nykko, CoReNtiN, ANd MAthiLde
foR hAviNg the couRAge to leAp iNto a secoNd cycle
ThANk you to DeNis ANd to eveRyoNe who
woRked oN this seRies both NeAR ANd fAR
—BANNisteR

To my two AdveNtuReRs, Léo & Noé
To SAbiNe, my WARRioR PRiNcess
To ANdRée—mAy IlmAhil light heR pAth
—Nykko

To MAthiLde ANd my PAReNts
—JAffRé

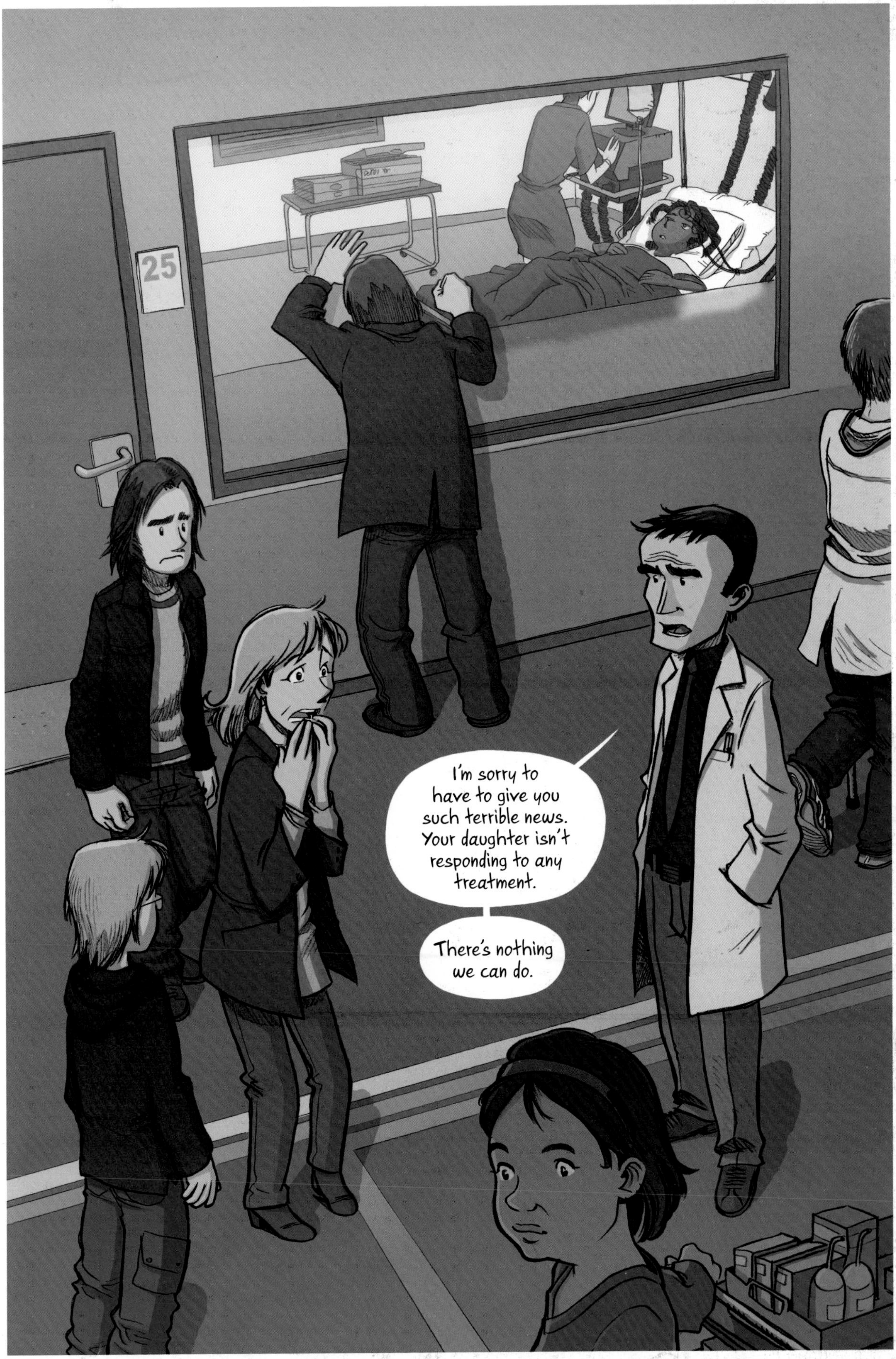
25
I'm sorry to have to give you such terrible news. Your daughter isn't responding to any treatment.
There's nothing we can do.

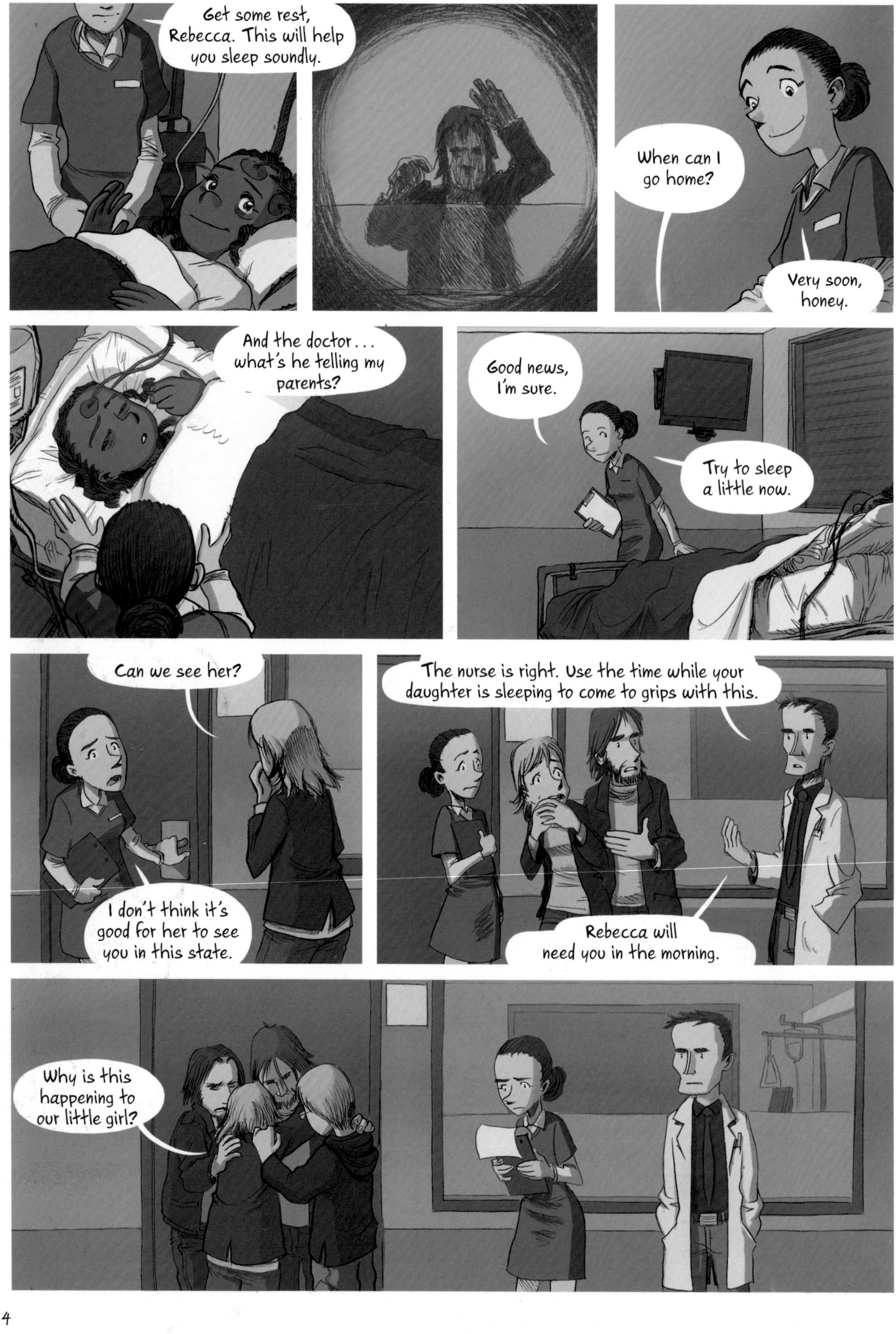
Get some rest, Rebecca. This will help you sleep soundly.
When can I go home?
Very soon, honey.
And the doctor... what's he telling my parents?
Good news, I'm sure.
Try to sleep a little now.
Can we see her?
I don't think it's good for her to see you in this state.
The nurse is right. Use the time while your daughter is sleeping to come to grips with this.
Rebecca will need you in the morning.
Why is this happening to our little girl?

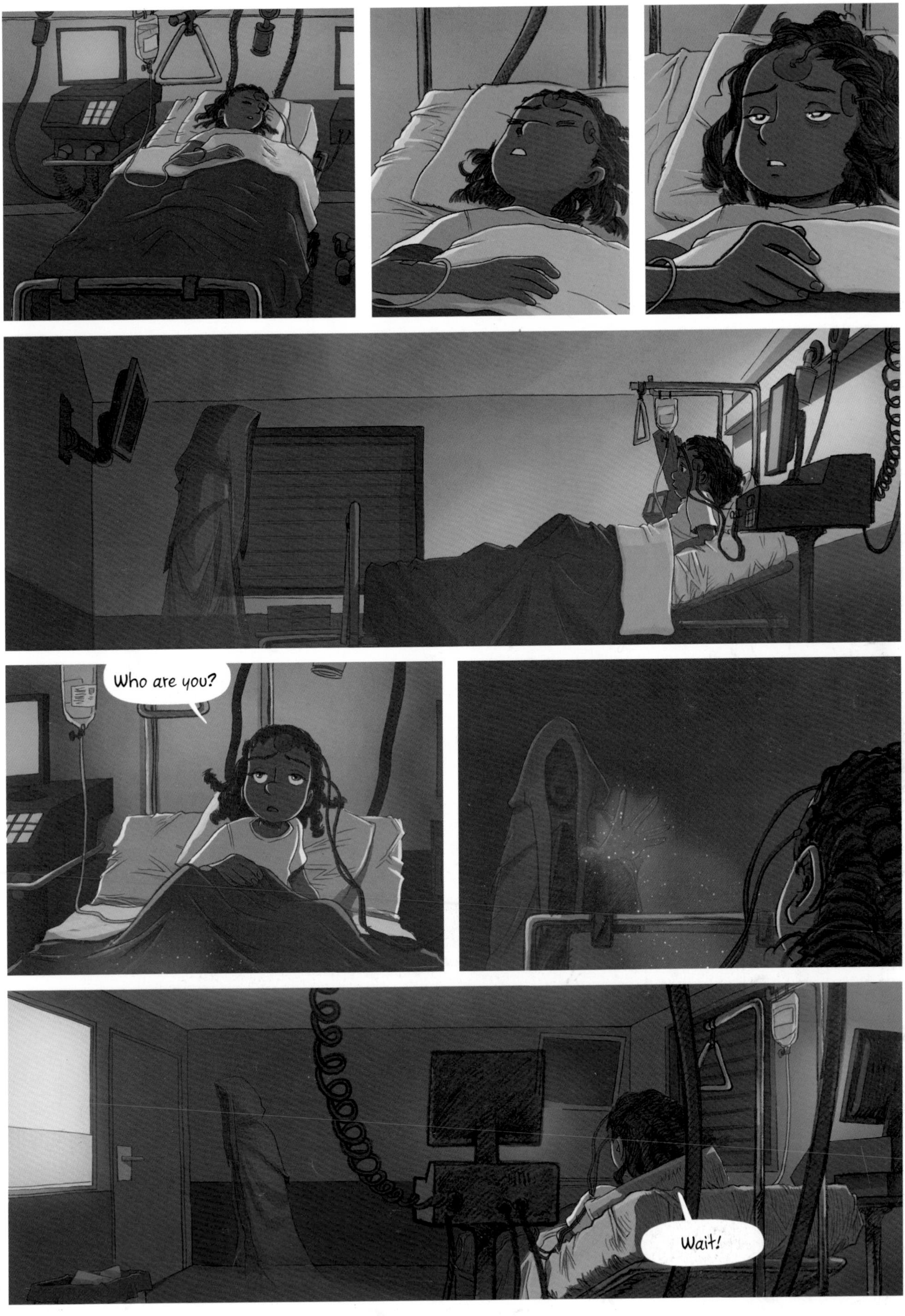
Who are you?
Wait!

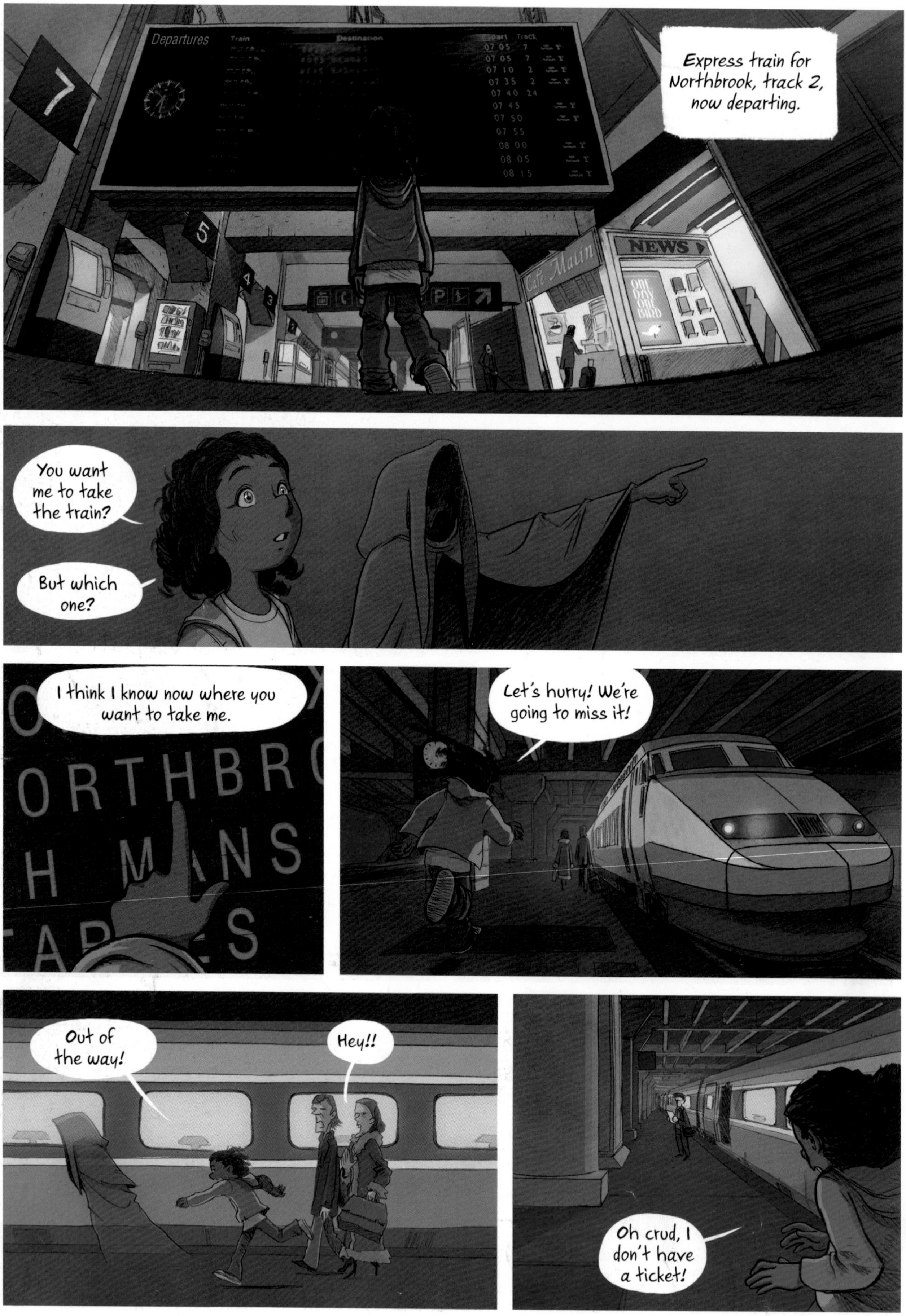
Departures
Express train for Northbrook, track 2, now departing.
NEWS
Café Malin
ONE DAY ONE BIRD
You want me to take the train?
But which one?
I think I know now where you want to take me.
ORTHBR
H MANS
Let's hurry! We're going to miss it!
Out of the way!
Hey!!
Oh crud, I don't have a ticket!

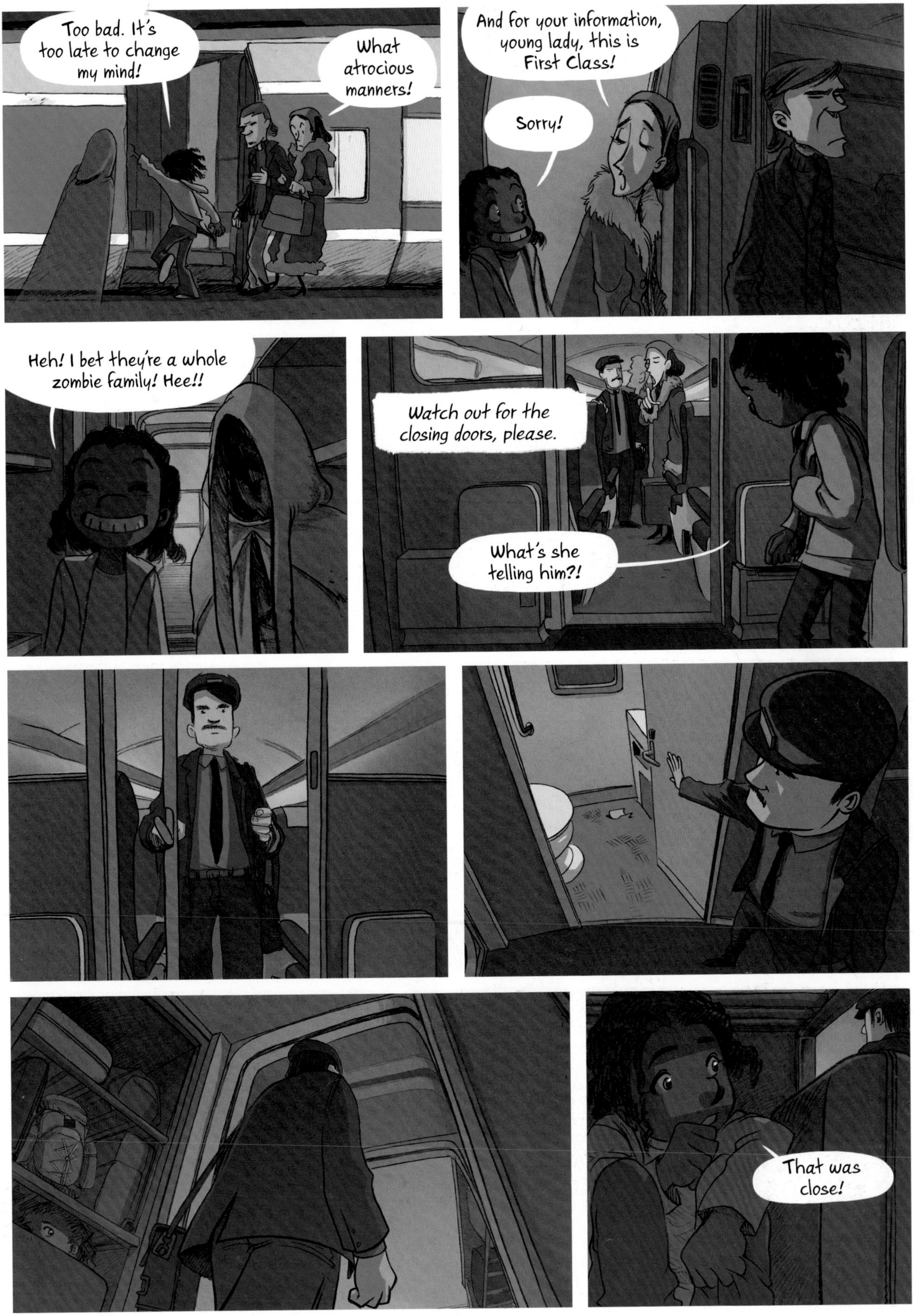
Too bad. It's too late to change my mind!
What atrocious manners!
And for your information, young lady, this is First Class!
Sorry!
Heh! I bet they're a whole zombie family! Hee!!
Watch out for the closing doors, please.
What's she telling him?!
That was close!

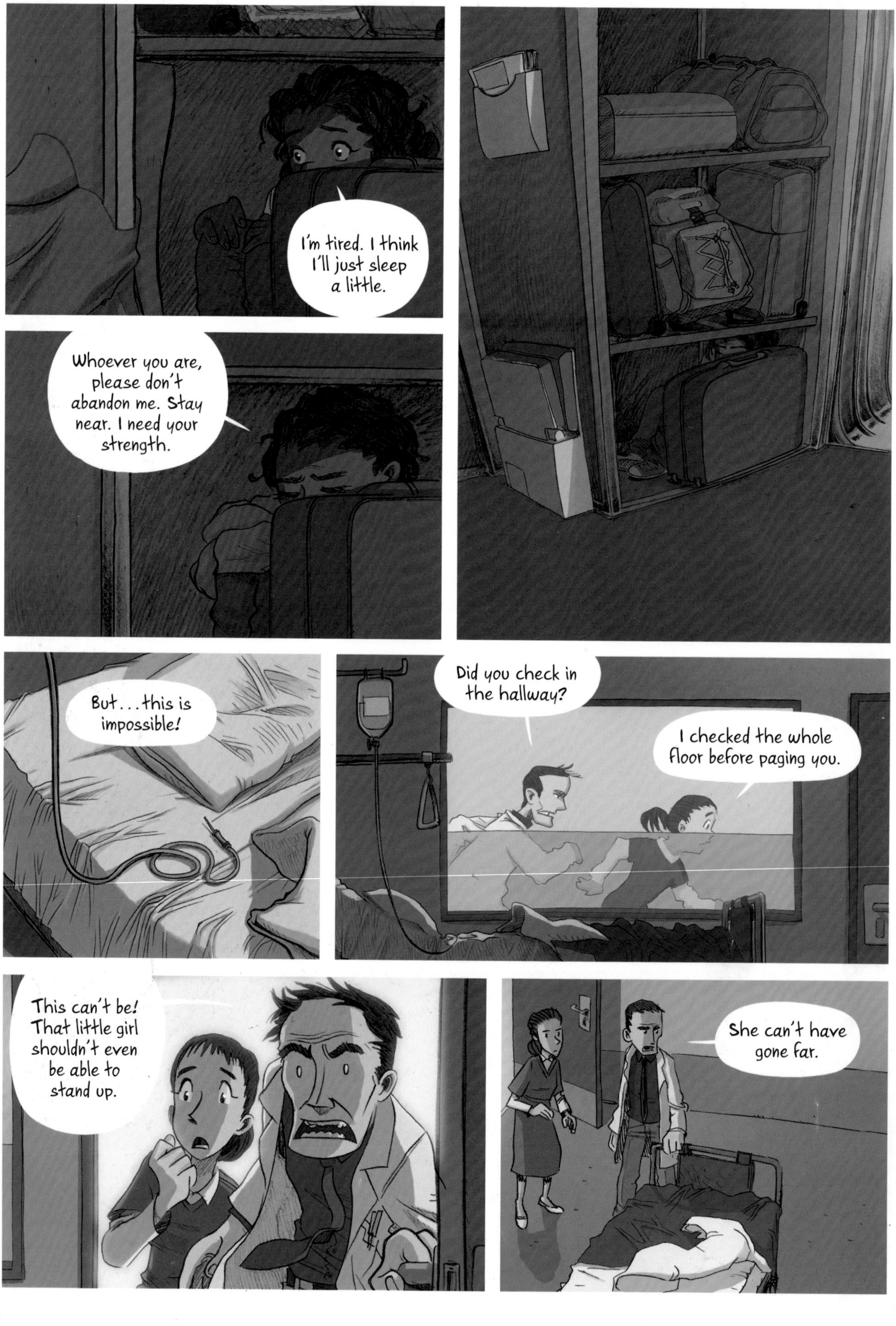
I'm tired. I think I'll just sleep a little.
Whoever you are, please don't abandon me. Stay near. I need your strength.
But . . . this is impossible!
Did you check in the hallway?
I checked the whole floor before paging you.
This can't be! That little girl shouldn't even be able to stand up.
She can't have gone far.

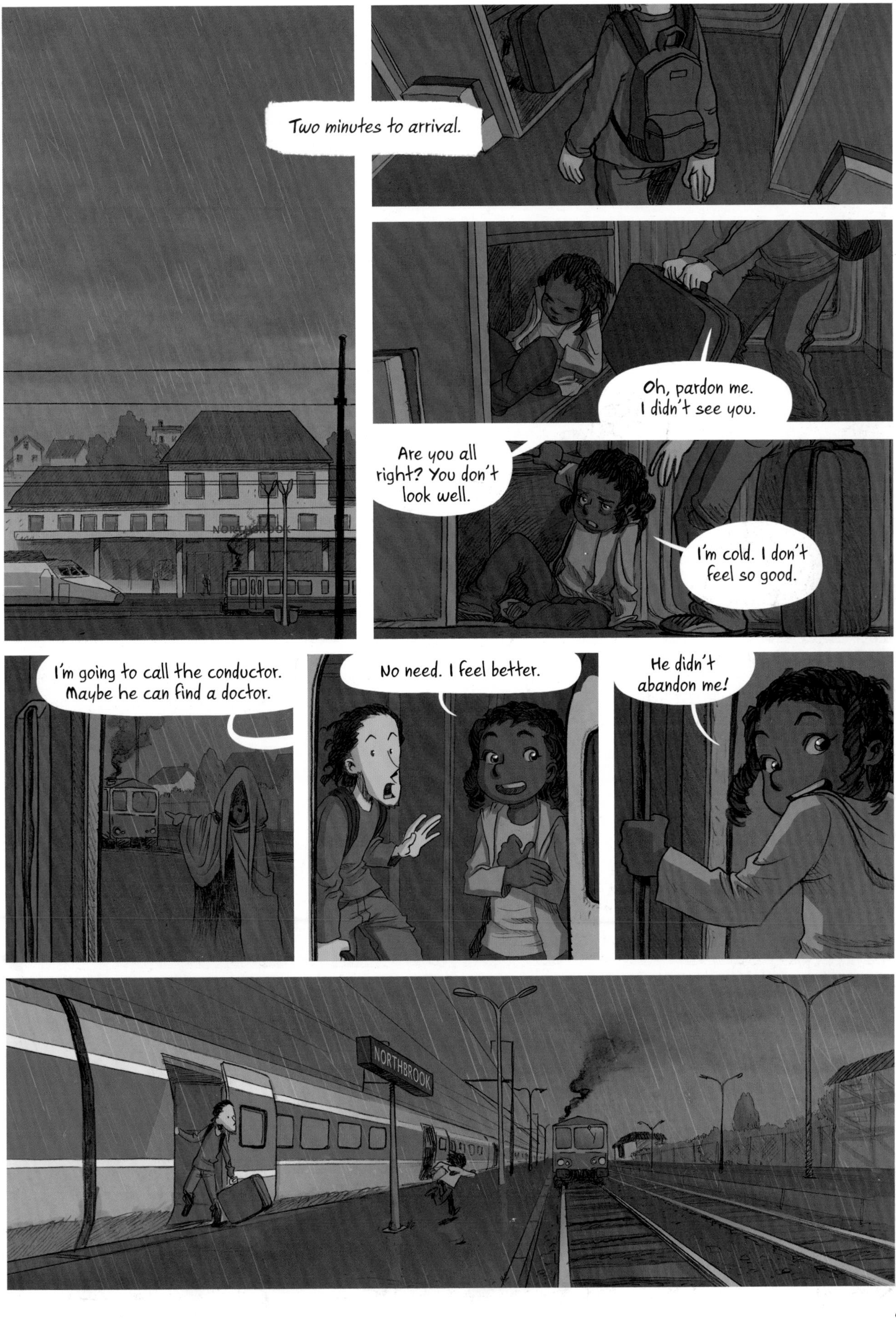
Two minutes to arrival.
NORTHBROOK
Oh, pardon me. I didn't see you.
Are you all right? You don't look well.
I'm cold. I don't feel so good.
I'm going to call the conductor. Maybe he can find a doctor.
No need. I feel better.
He didn't abandon me!
NORTHBROOK

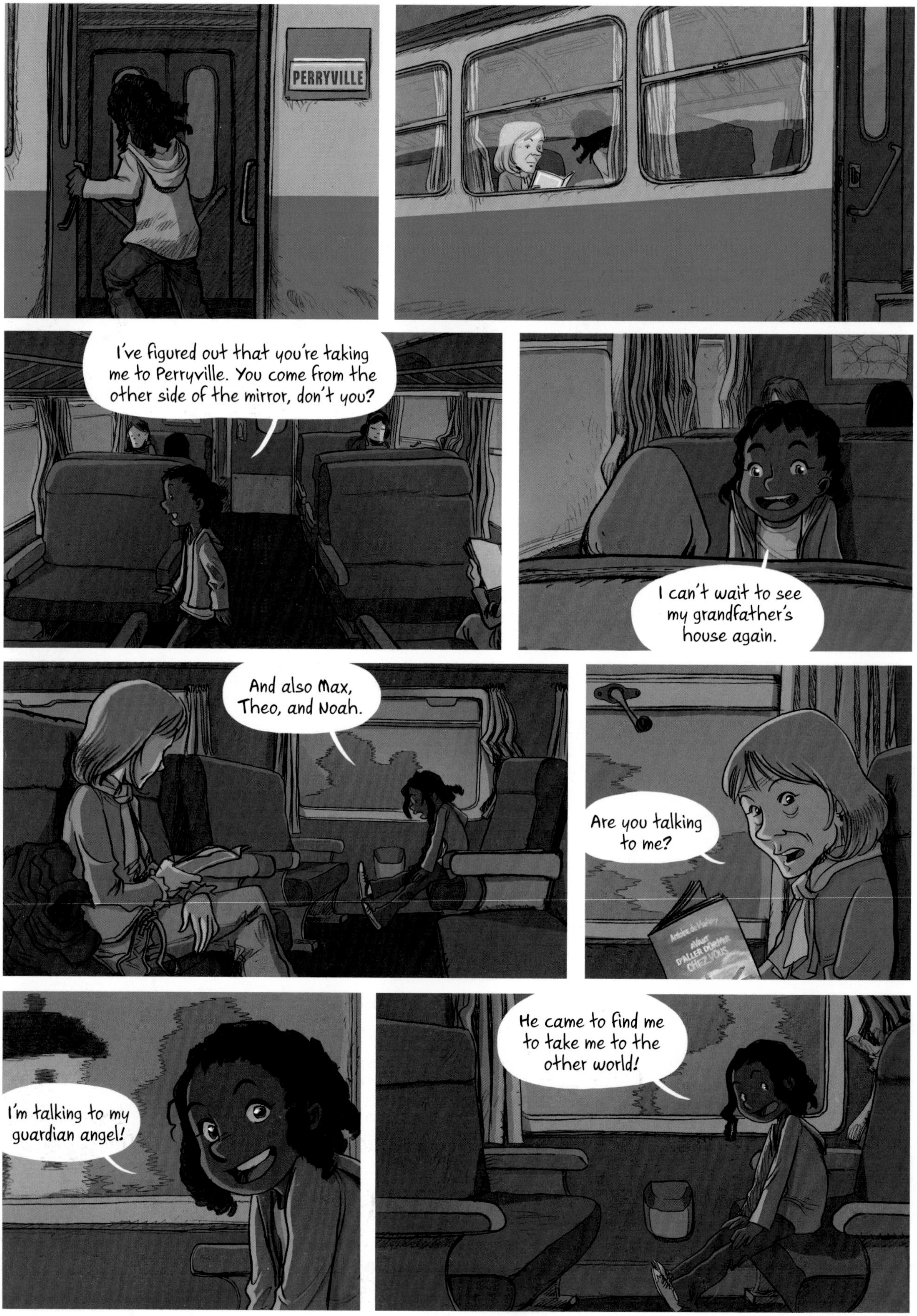
PERRYVILLE
I've figured out that you're taking me to Perryville. You come from the other side of the mirror, don't you?
I can't wait to see my grandfather's house again.
And also Max, Theo, and Noah.
Are you talking to me?
I'm talking to my guardian angel!
He came to find me to take me to the other world!

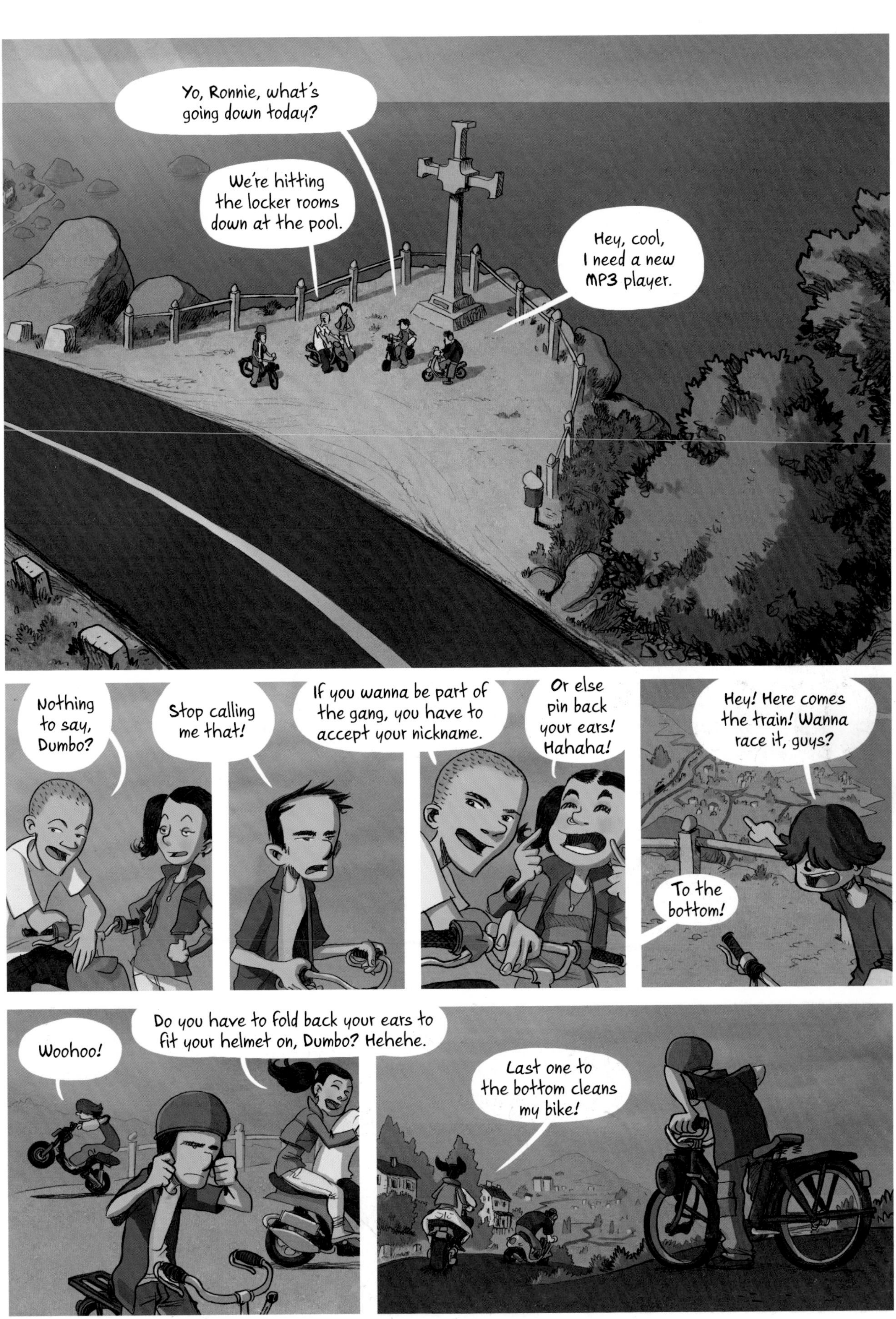

Yo, Ronnie, what's going down today?
We're hitting the locker rooms down at the pool.
Hey, cool, I need a new MP3 player.
Nothing to say, Dumbo?
Stop calling me that!
If you wanna be part of the gang, you have to accept your nickname.
Or else pin back your ears! Hahaha!
Hey! Here comes the train! Wanna race it, guys?
To the bottom!
Woohoo!
Do you have to fold back your ears to fit your helmet on, Dumbo? Hehehe.
Last one to the bottom cleans my bike!

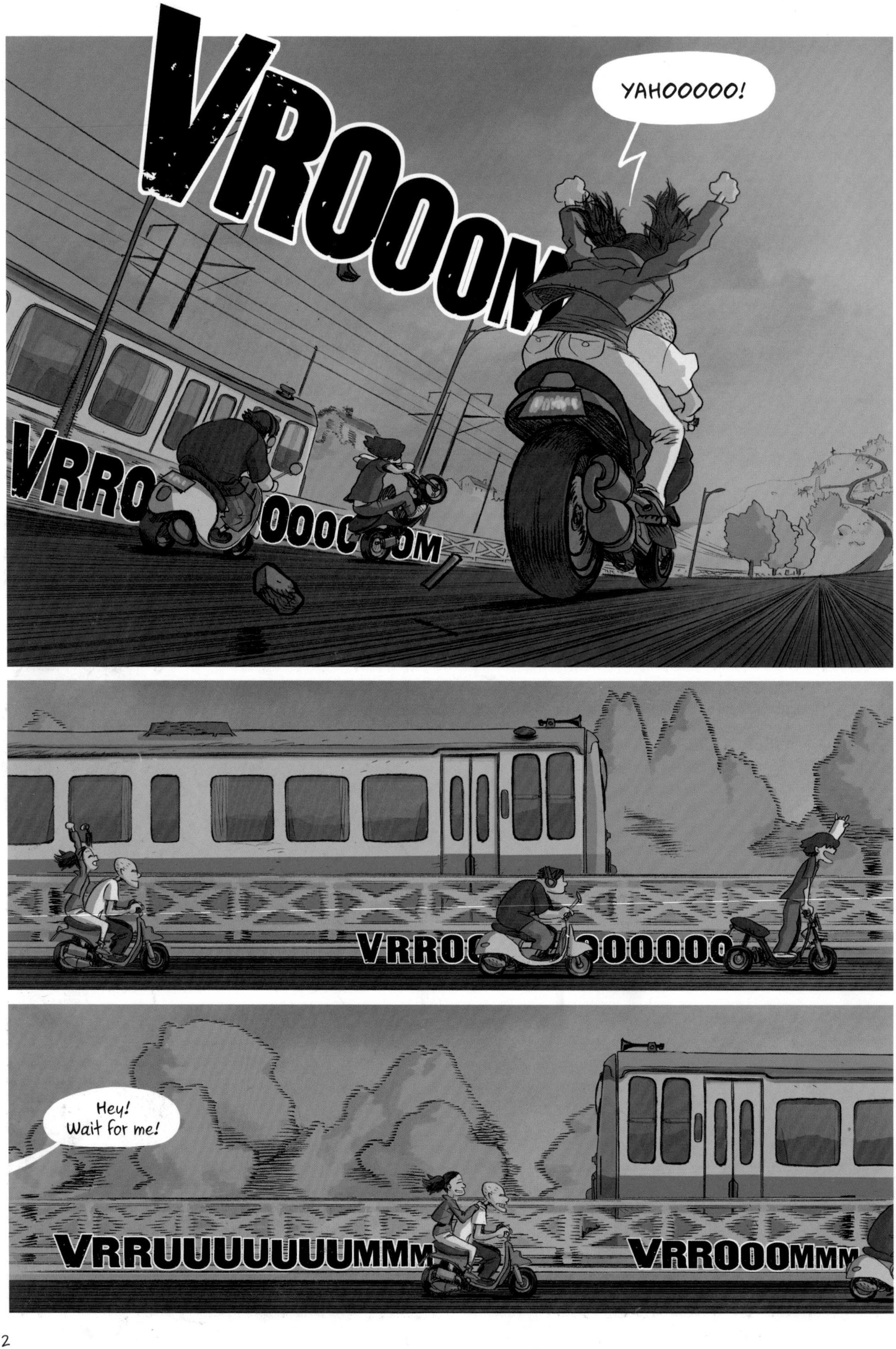
VROOOOM
YAHOOOOO!
VRROOOOOOOM
VRROOOOOOOOO
Hey! Wait for me!
VRRUUUUUUUMMM
VRROOOMMM

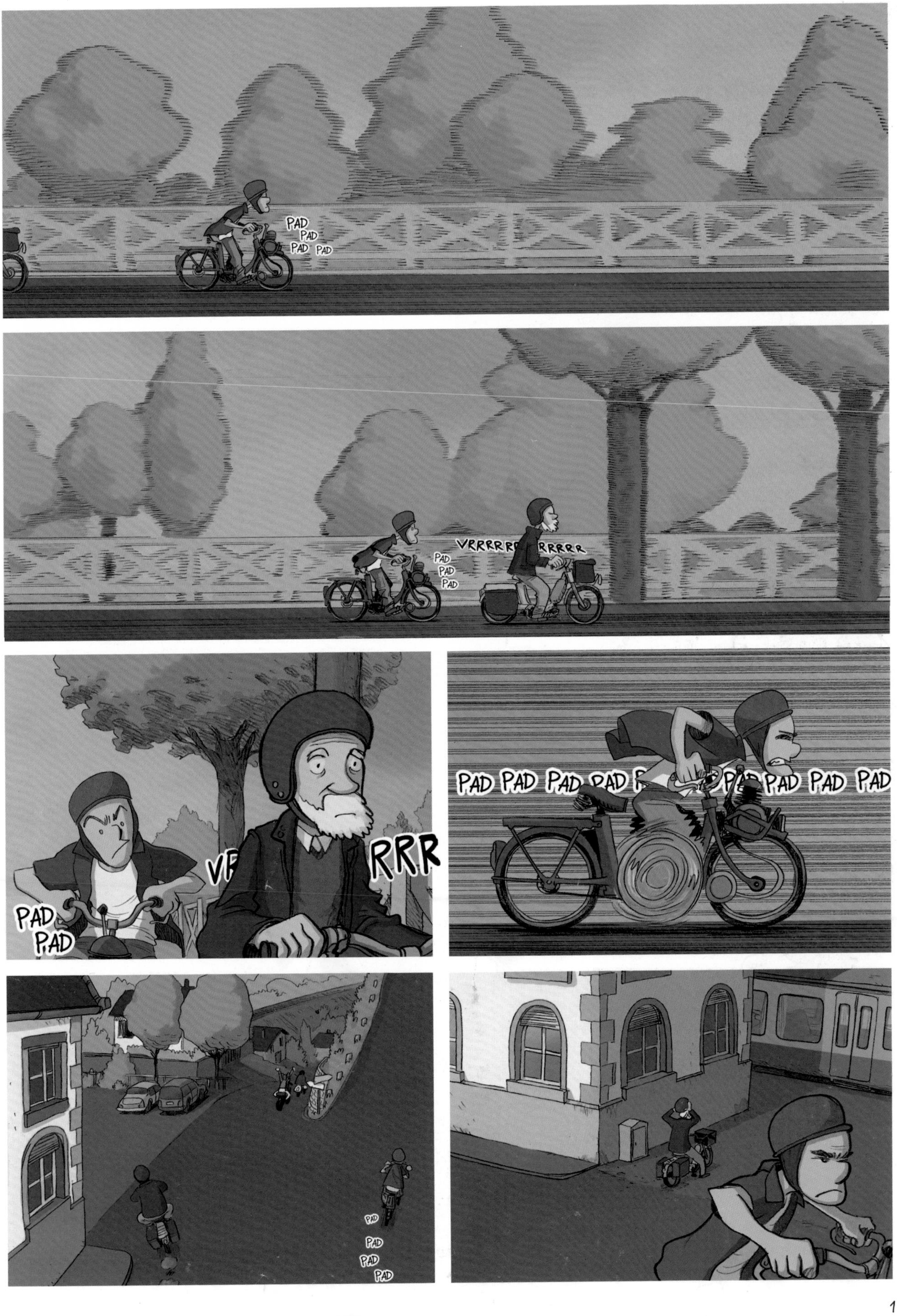
PAD
PAD
PAD PAD
VRRRRRRRRRRRR
PAD
PAD
PAD
PAD
PAD
VR
RRR
PAD PAD PAD PAD
PAD PAD PAD
PAD
PAD
PAD
PAD

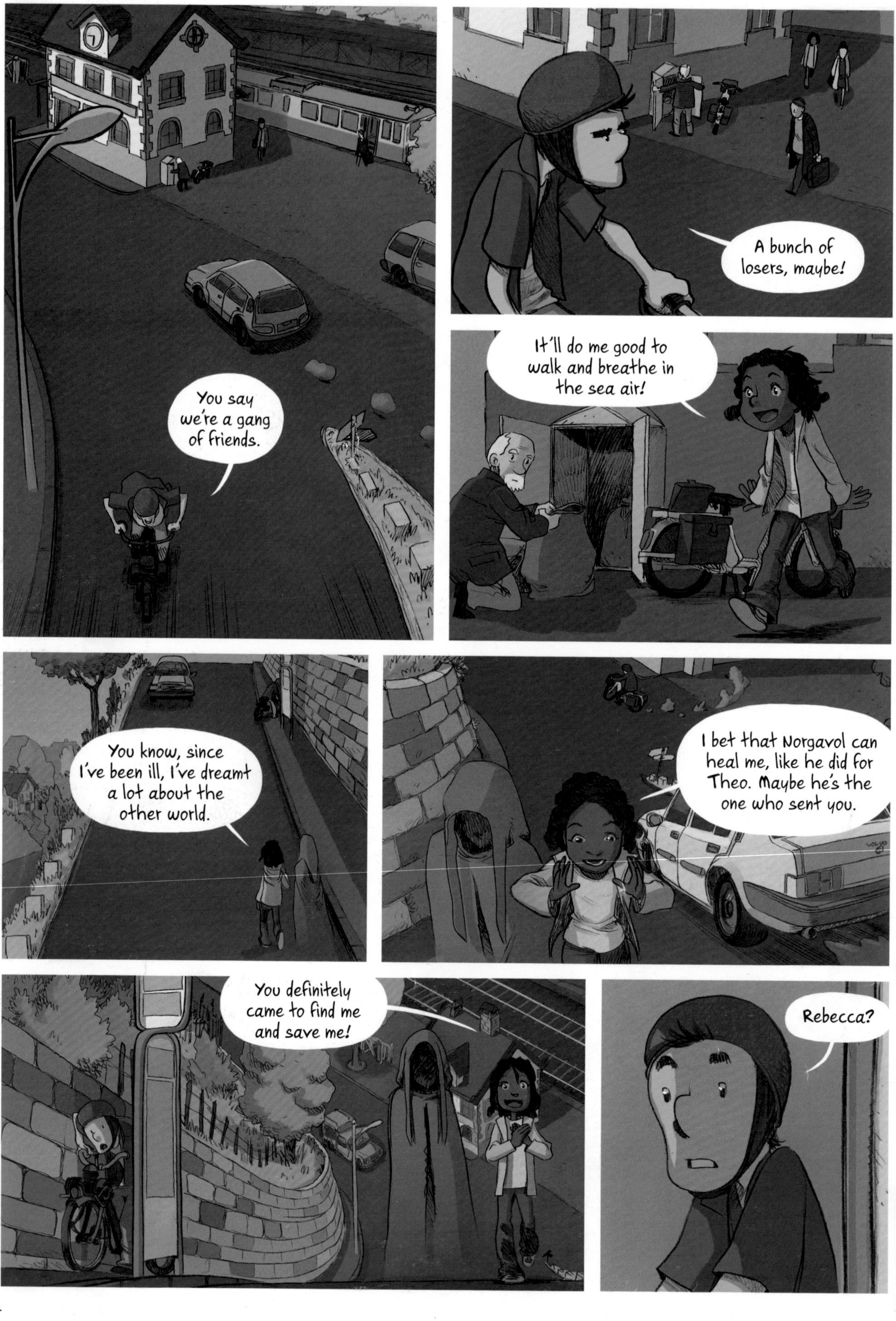
You say we're a gang of friends.
A bunch of losers, maybe!
It'll do me good to walk and breathe in the sea air!
You know, since I've been ill, I've dreamt a lot about the other world.
I bet that Norgavol can heal me, like he did for Theo. Maybe he's the one who sent you.
You definitely came to find me and save me!
Rebecca?

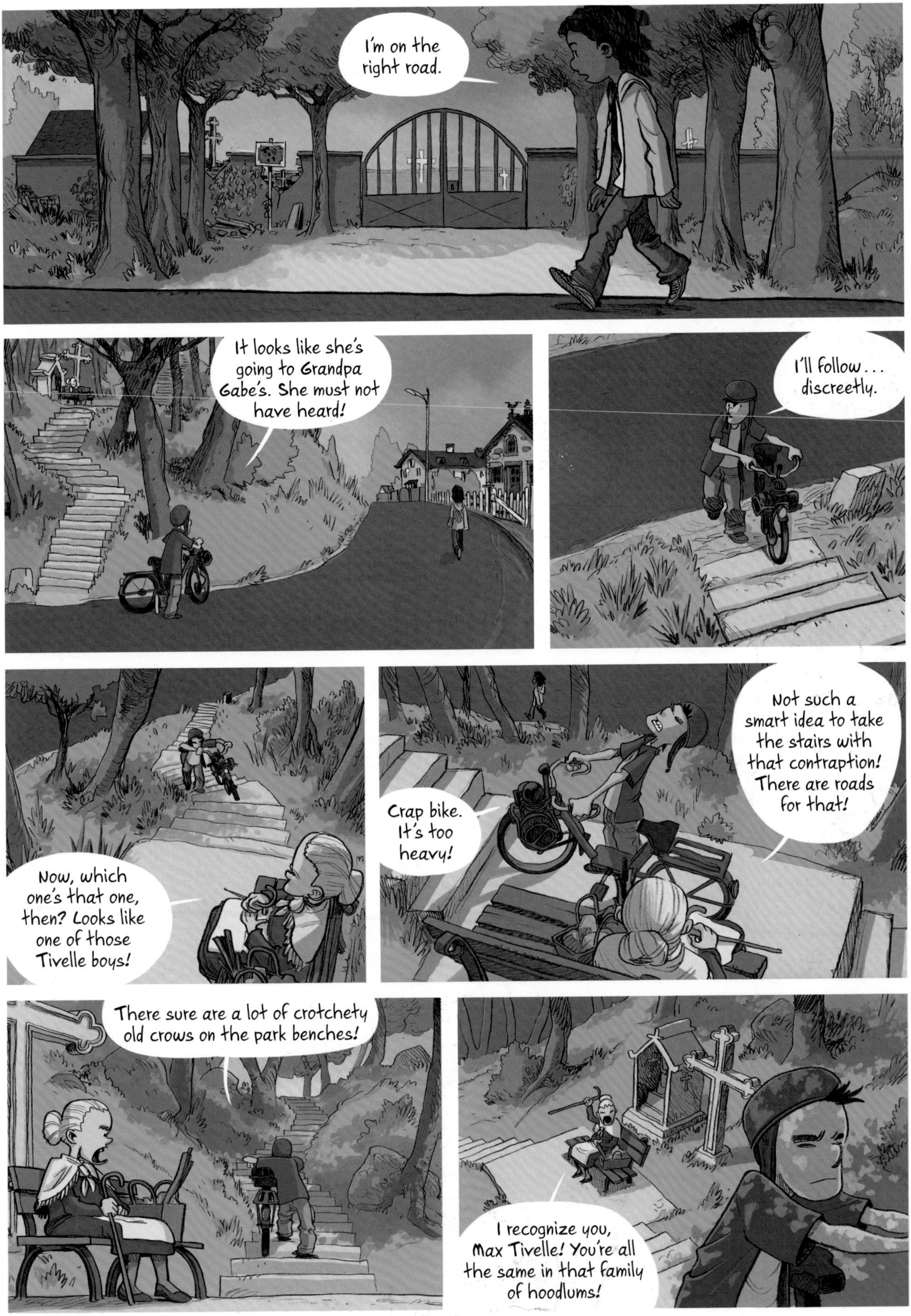
I'm on the right road.
It looks like she's going to Grandpa Gabe's. She must not have heard!
I'll follow . . . discreetly.
Now, which one's that one, then? Looks like one of those Tivelle boys!
Crap bike. It's too heavy!
Not such a smart idea to take the stairs with that contraption! There are roads for that!
There sure are a lot of crotchety old crows on the park benches!
I recognize you, Max Tivelle! You're all the same in that family of hoodlums!

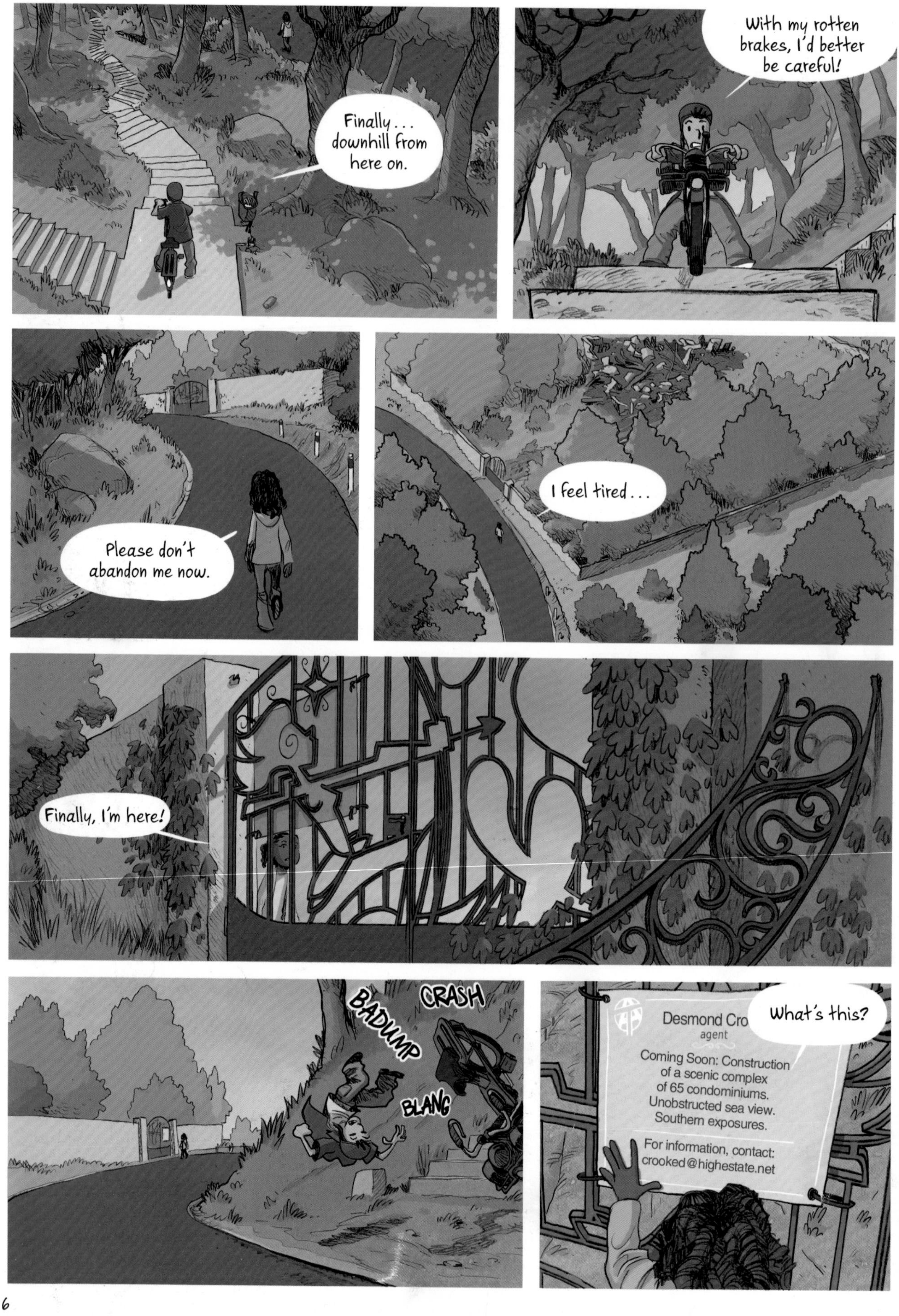
Finally... downhill from here on.
With my rotten brakes, I'd better be careful!
Please don't abandon me now.
I feel tired...
Finally, I'm here!
BADUMP
CRASH
BLANG
Desmond Cro
agent
Coming Soon: Construction of a scenic complex of 65 condominiums. Unobstructed sea view. Southern exposures.
For information, contact: crooked@highestate.net
What's this?

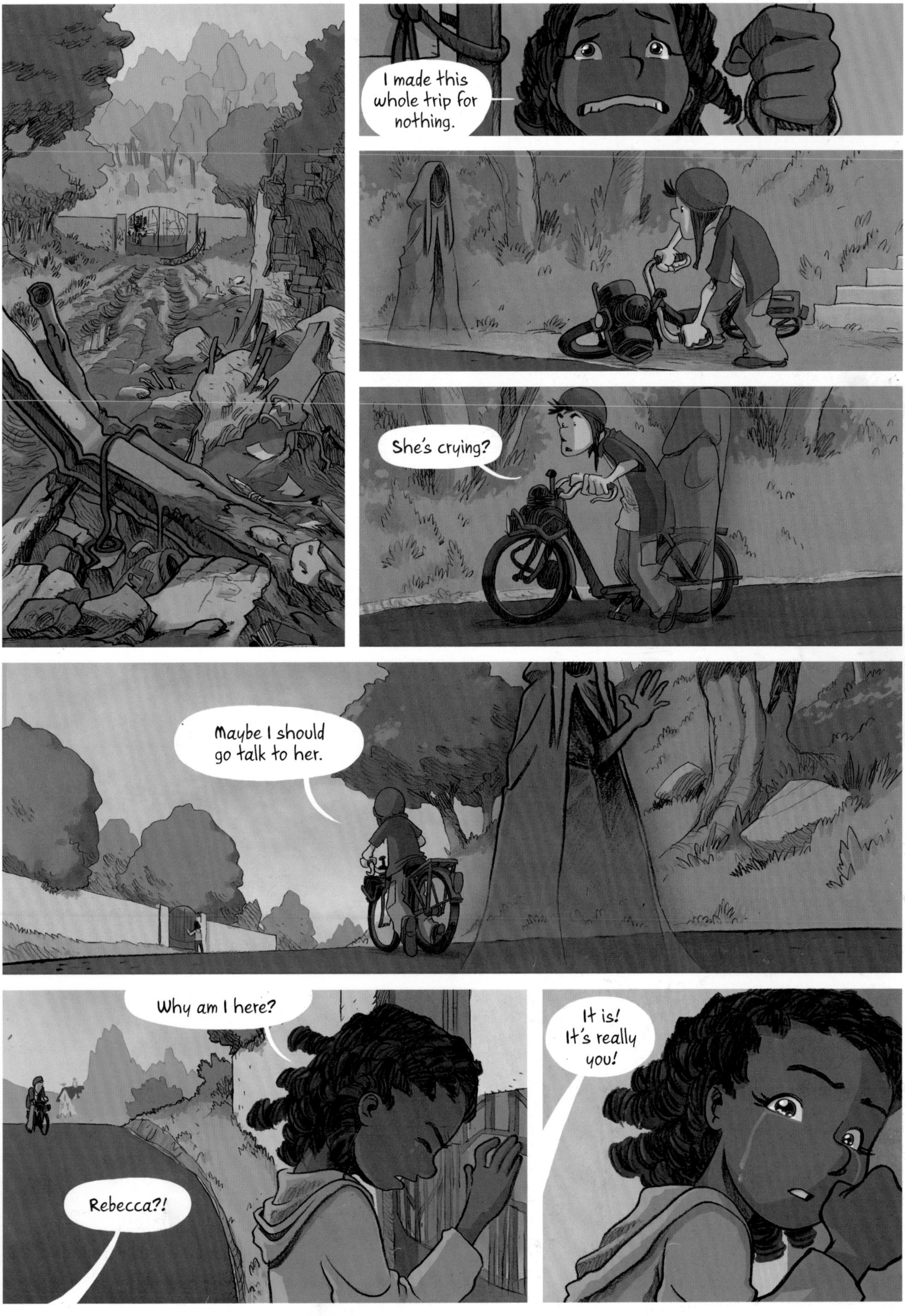
I made this whole trip for nothing.
She's crying?
Maybe I should go talk to her.
Why am I here?
Rebecca?!
It is! It's really you!

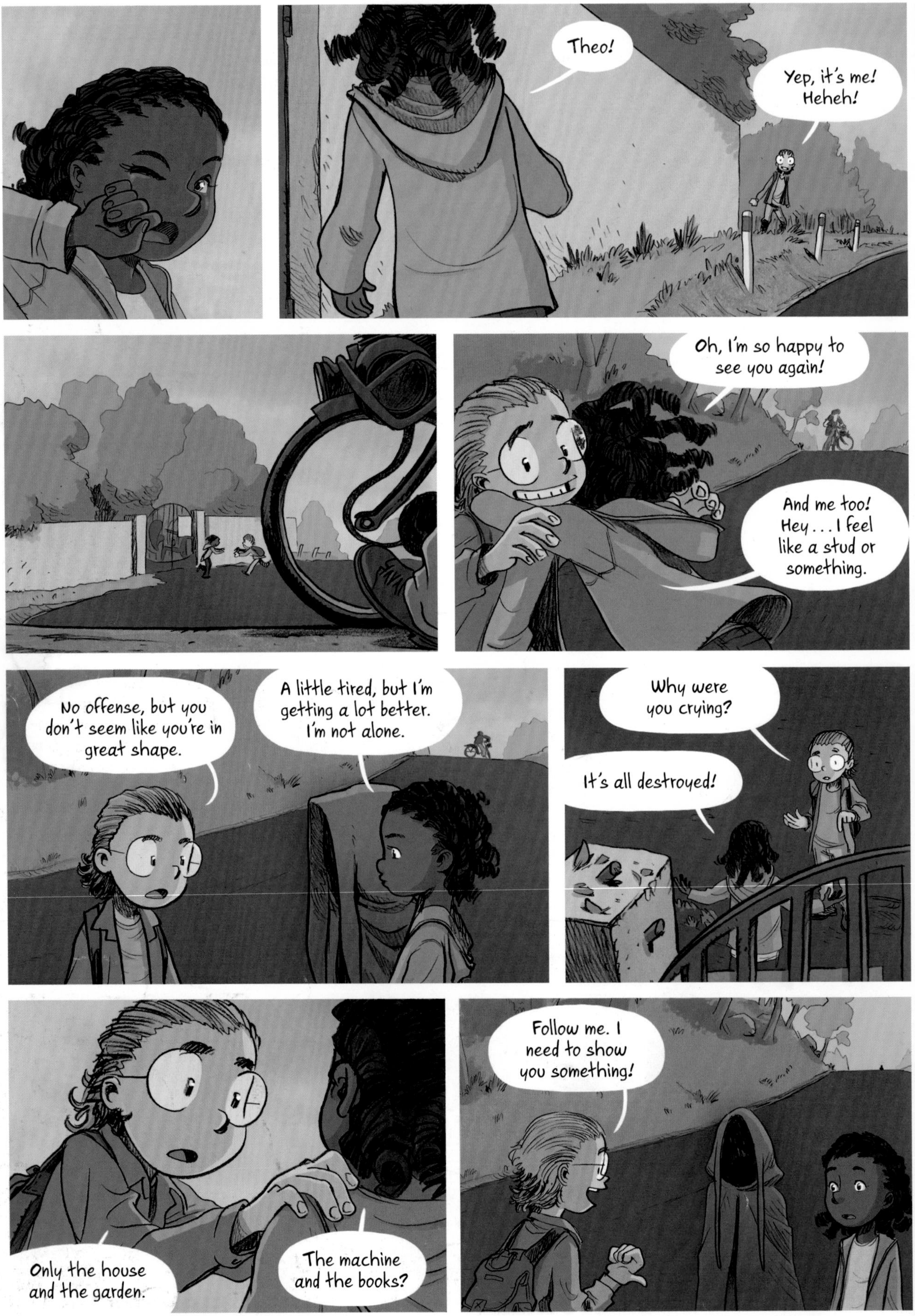
Theo!
Yep, it's me! Heheh!
Oh, I'm so happy to see you again!
And me too! Hey . . . I feel like a stud or something.
No offense, but you don't seem like you're in great shape.
A little tired, but I'm getting a lot better. I'm not alone.
Why were you crying?
It's all destroyed!
Only the house and the garden.
The machine and the books?
Follow me. I need to show you something!

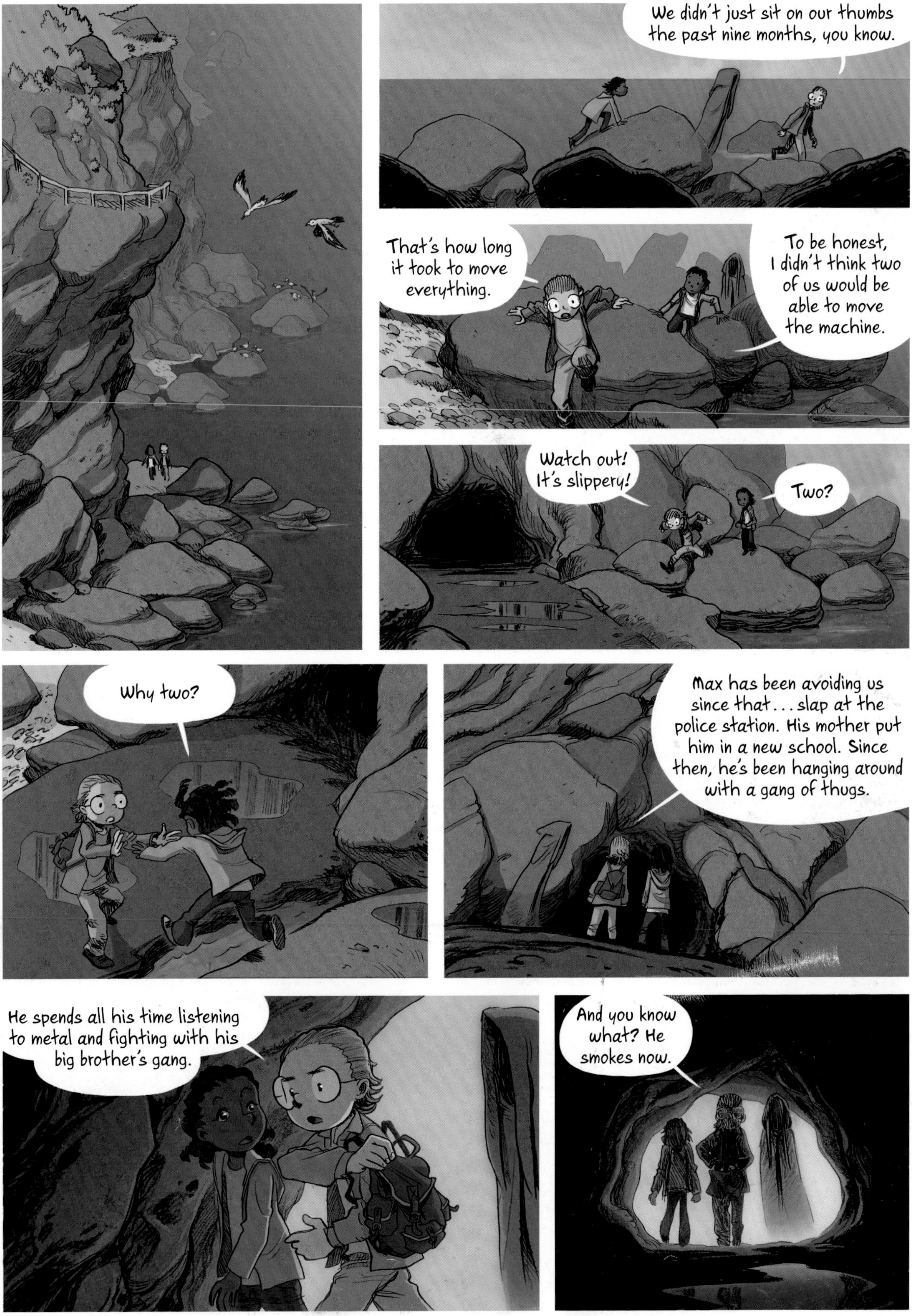

We didn't just sit on our thumbs the past nine months, you know.
That's how long it took to move everything.
To be honest, I didn't think two of us would be able to move the machine.
Watch out! It's slippery!
Two?
Why two?
Max has been avoiding us since that... slap at the police station. His mother put him in a new school. Since then, he's been hanging around with a gang of thugs.
He spends all his time listening to metal and fighting with his big brother's gang.
And you know what? He smokes now.

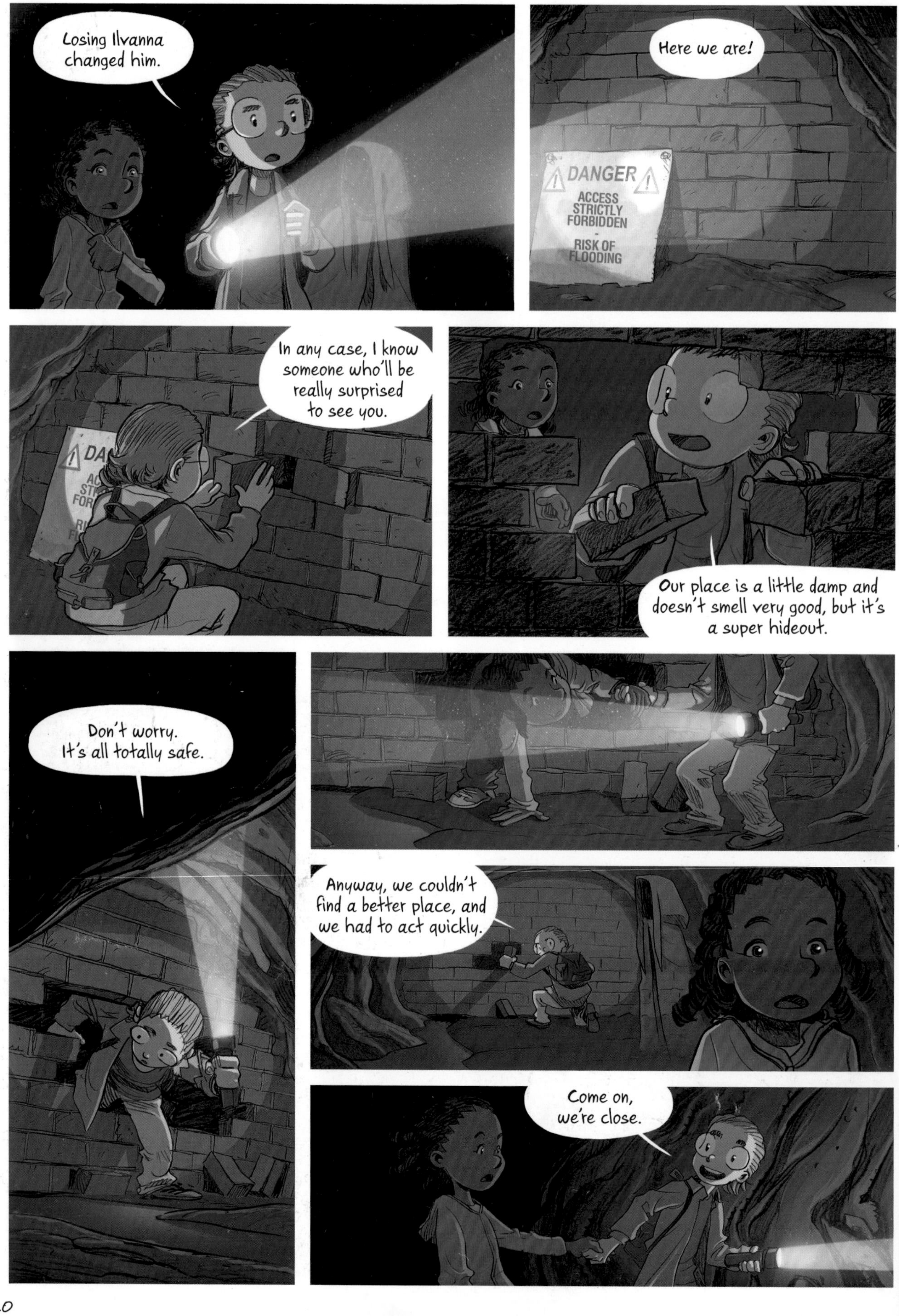

Losing Ilvanna changed him.
Here we are!
DANGER
ACCESS STRICTLY FORBIDDEN
-
RISK OF FLOODING
In any case, I know someone who'll be really surprised to see you.
Our place is a little damp and doesn't smell very good, but it's a super hideout.
Don't worry. It's all totally safe.
Anyway, we couldn't find a better place, and we had to act quickly.
Come on, we're close.

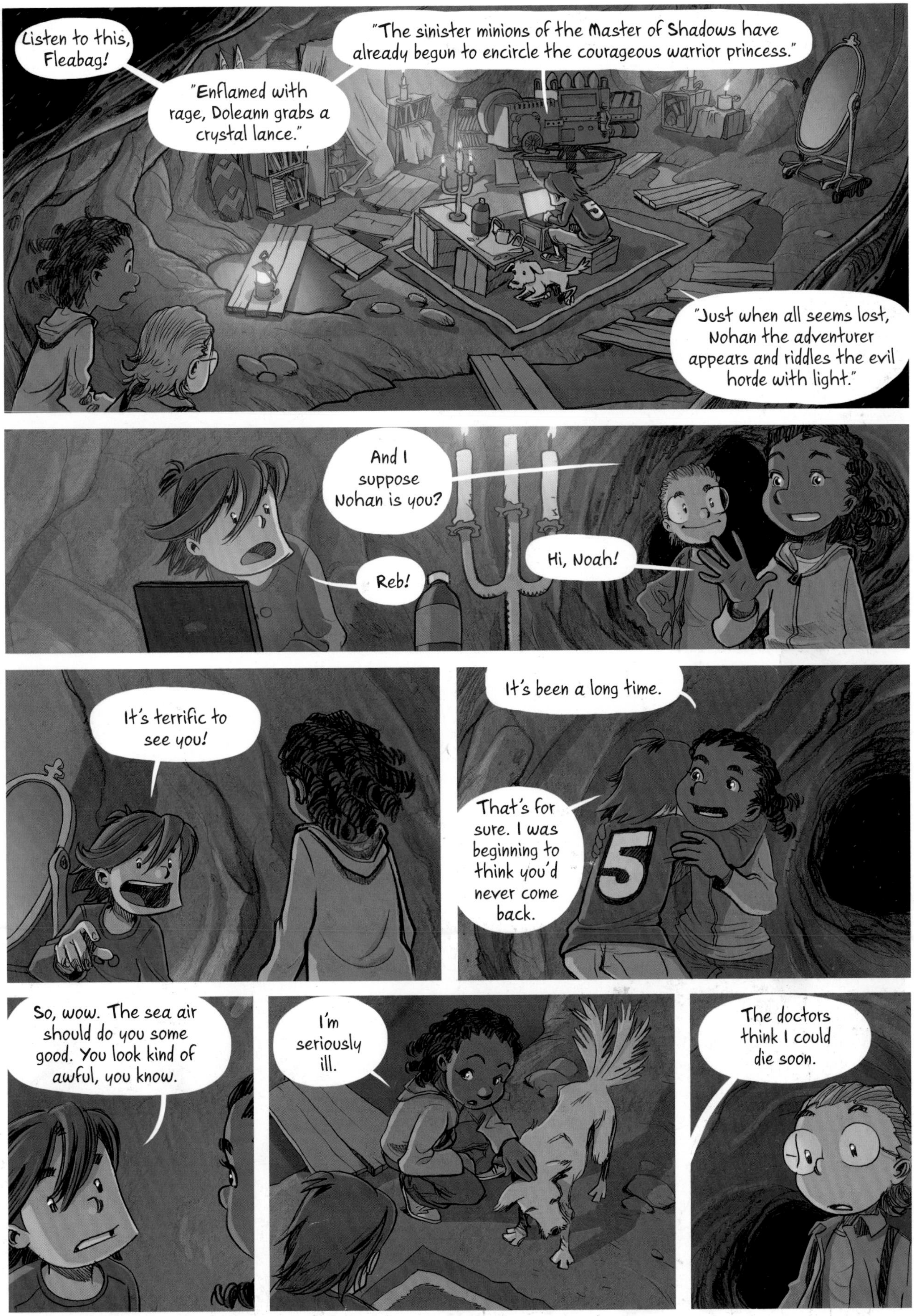
Listen to this, Fleabag!
"Enflamed with rage, Doleann grabs a crystal lance."
"The sinister minions of the Master of Shadows have already begun to encircle the courageous warrior princess."
"Just when all seems lost, Nohan the adventurer appears and riddles the evil horde with light."
And I suppose Nohan is you?
Reb!
Hi, Noah!
It's terrific to see you!
It's been a long time.
That's for sure. I was beginning to think you'd never come back.
So, wow. The sea air should do you some good. You look kind of awful, you know.
I'm seriously ill.
The doctors think I could die soon.

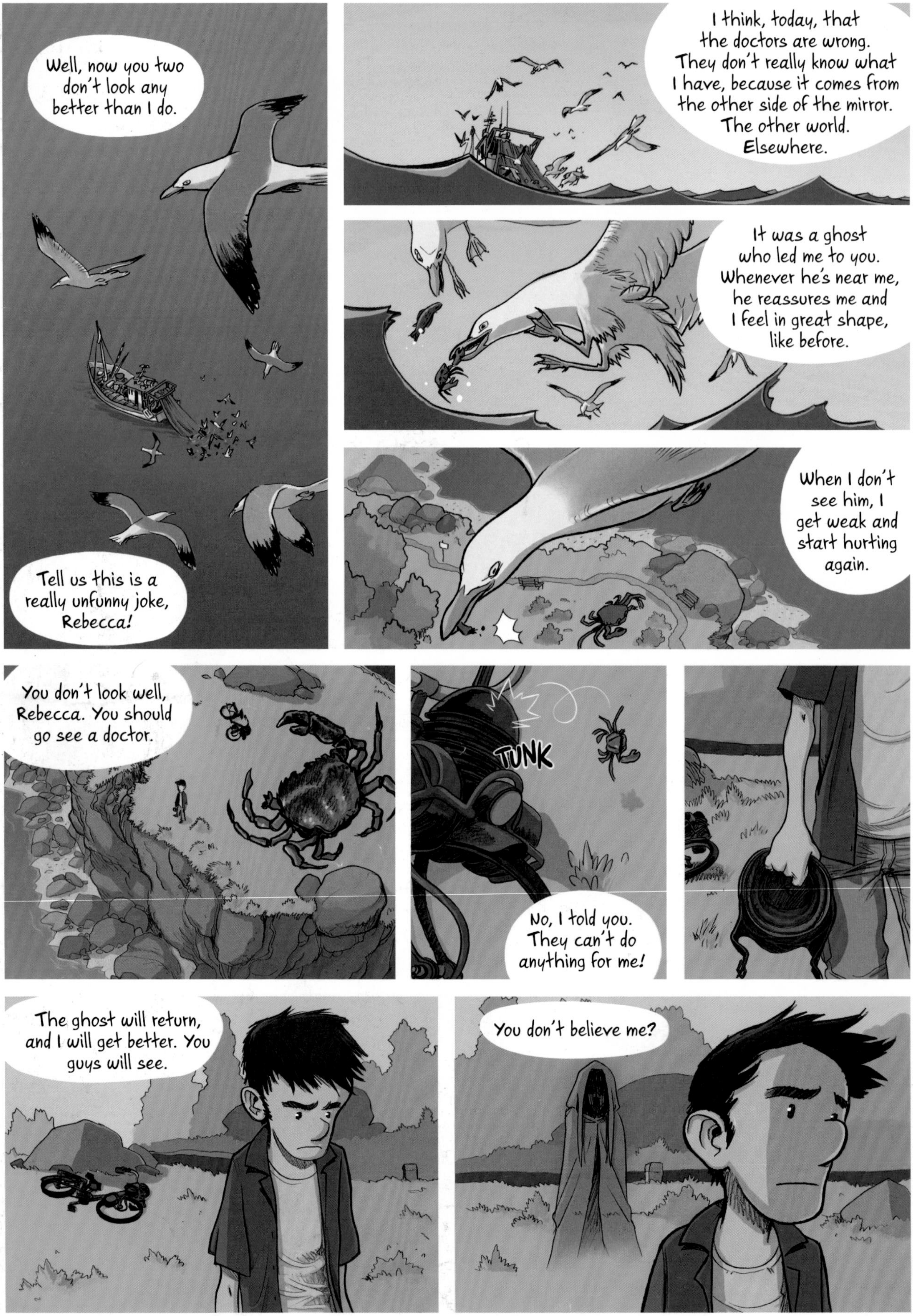

Well, now you two don't look any better than I do.
Tell us this is a really unfunny joke, Rebecca!
I think, today, that the doctors are wrong. They don't really know what I have, because it comes from the other side of the mirror. The other world. Elsewhere.
It was a ghost who led me to you. Whenever he's near me, he reassures me and I feel in great shape, like before.
When I don't see him, I get weak and start hurting again.
You don't look well, Rebecca. You should go see a doctor.
TUNK
No, I told you. They can't do anything for me!
The ghost will return, and I will get better. You guys will see.
You don't believe me?

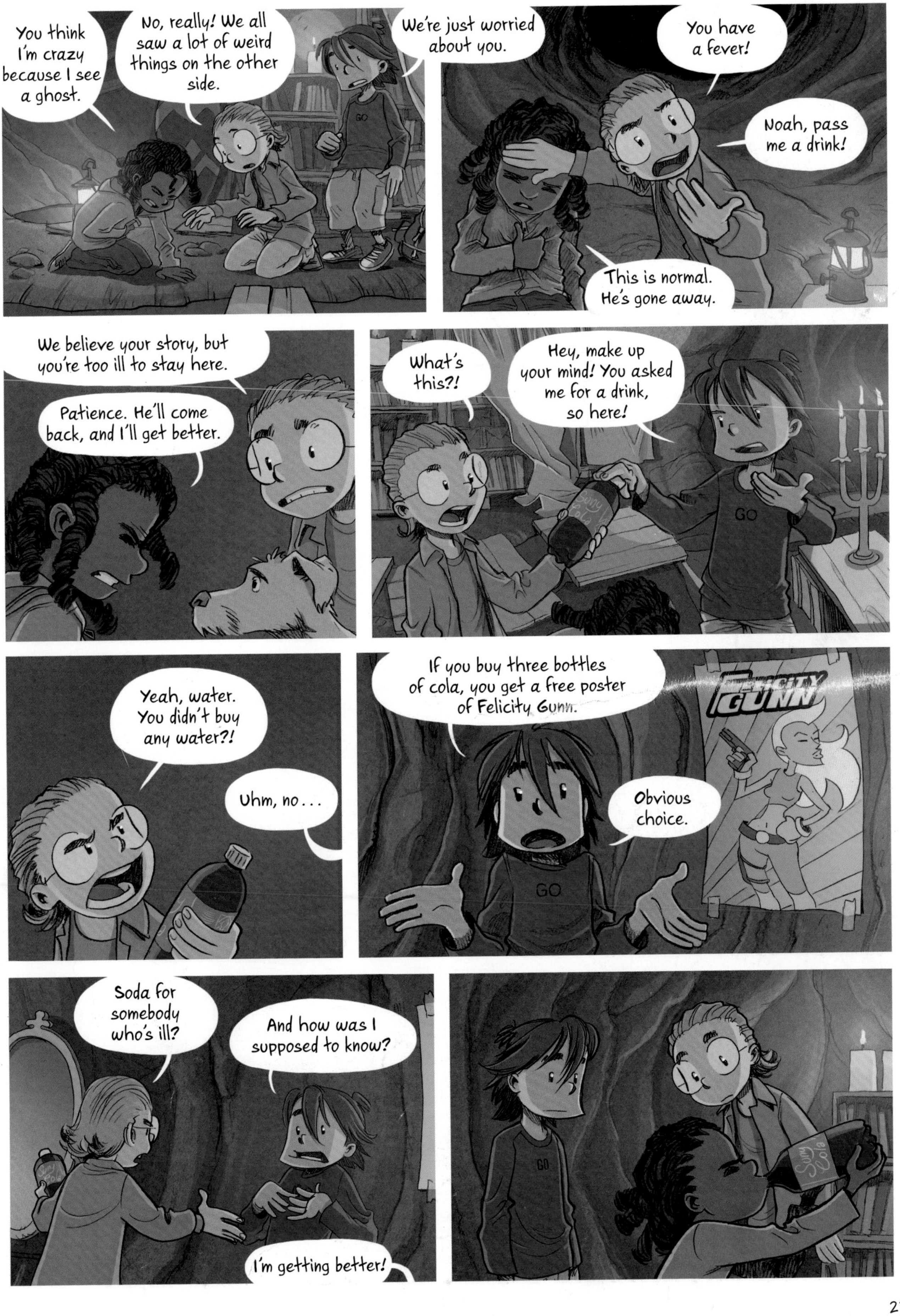
You think I'm crazy because I see a ghost.
No, really! We all saw a lot of weird things on the other side.
We're just worried about you.
You have a fever!
Noah, pass me a drink!
This is normal. He's gone away.
We believe your story, but you're too ill to stay here.
Patience. He'll come back, and I'll get better.
What's this?!
Hey, make up your mind! You asked me for a drink, so here!
Yeah, water. You didn't buy any water?!
Uhm, no...
If you buy three bottles of cola, you get a free poster of Felicity Gunn.
Obvious choice.
FELICITY GUNN
Soda for somebody who's ill?
And how was I supposed to know?
I'm getting better!

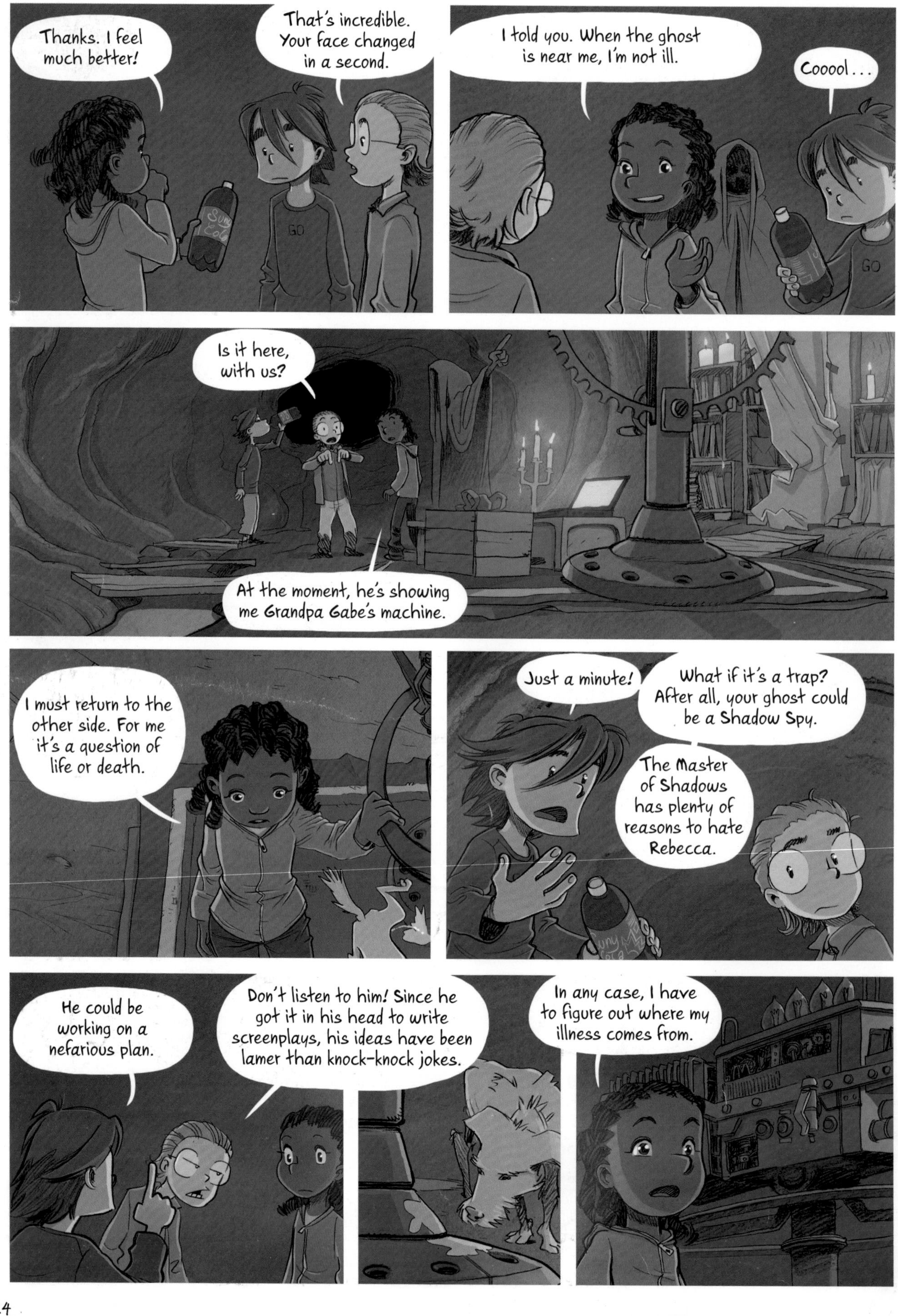
Thanks. I feel much better!
That's incredible. Your face changed in a second.
I told you. When the ghost is near me, I'm not ill.
Cooool...
Is it here, with us?
At the moment, he's showing me Grandpa Gabe's machine.
I must return to the other side. For me it's a question of life or death.
Just a minute!
What if it's a trap? After all, your ghost could be a Shadow Spy.
The Master of Shadows has plenty of reasons to hate Rebecca.
He could be working on a nefarious plan.
Don't listen to him! Since he got it in his head to write screenplays, his ideas have been lamer than knock-knock jokes.
In any case, I have to figure out where my illness comes from.

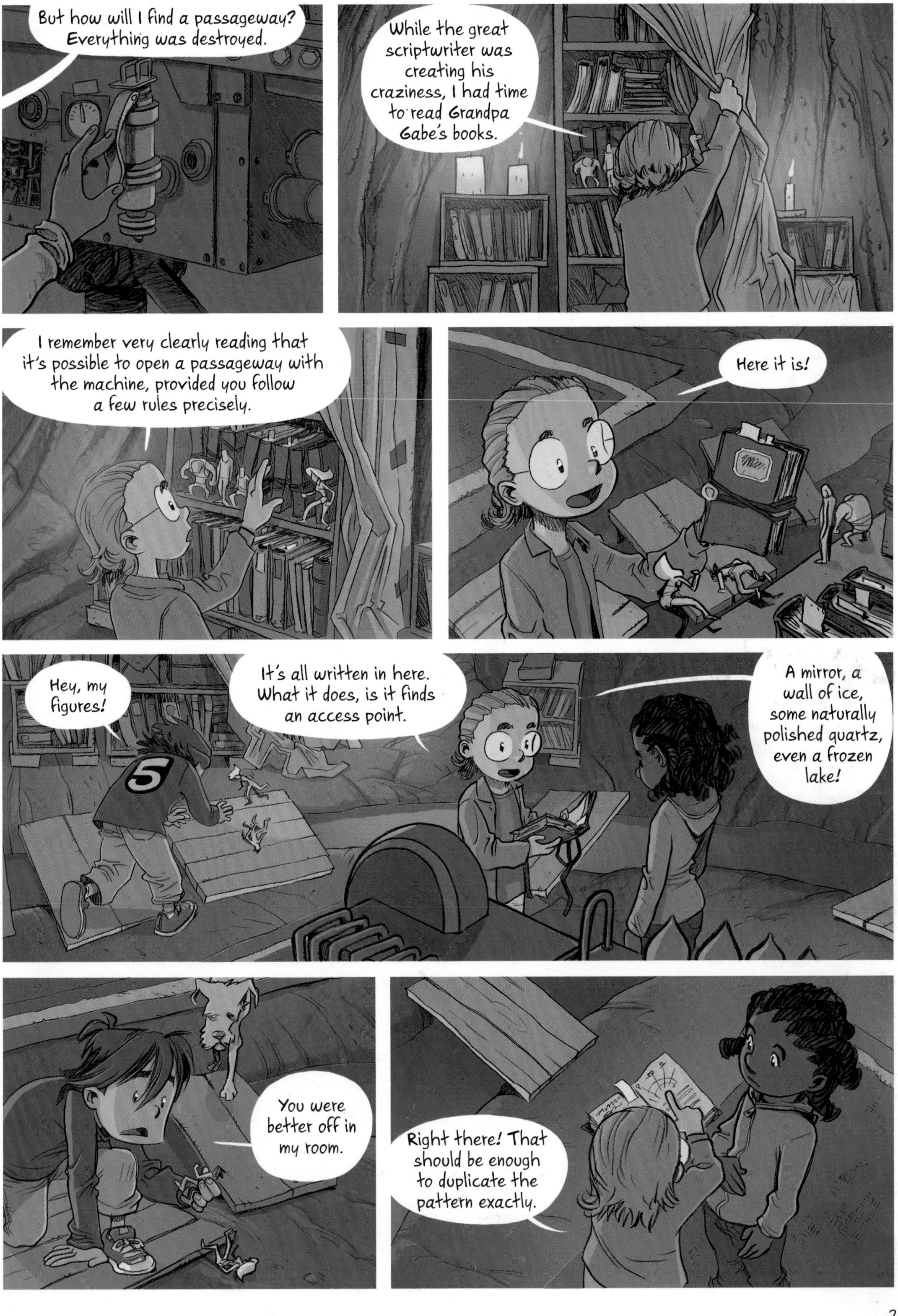
But how will I find a passageway? Everything was destroyed.
While the great scriptwriter was creating his craziness, I had time to read Grandpa Gabe's books.
I remember very clearly reading that it's possible to open a passageway with the machine, provided you follow a few rules precisely.
Here it is!
Hey, my figures!
It's all written in here. What it does, is it finds an access point.
A mirror, a wall of ice, some naturally polished quartz, even a frozen lake!
You were better off in my room.
Right there! That should be enough to duplicate the pattern exactly.

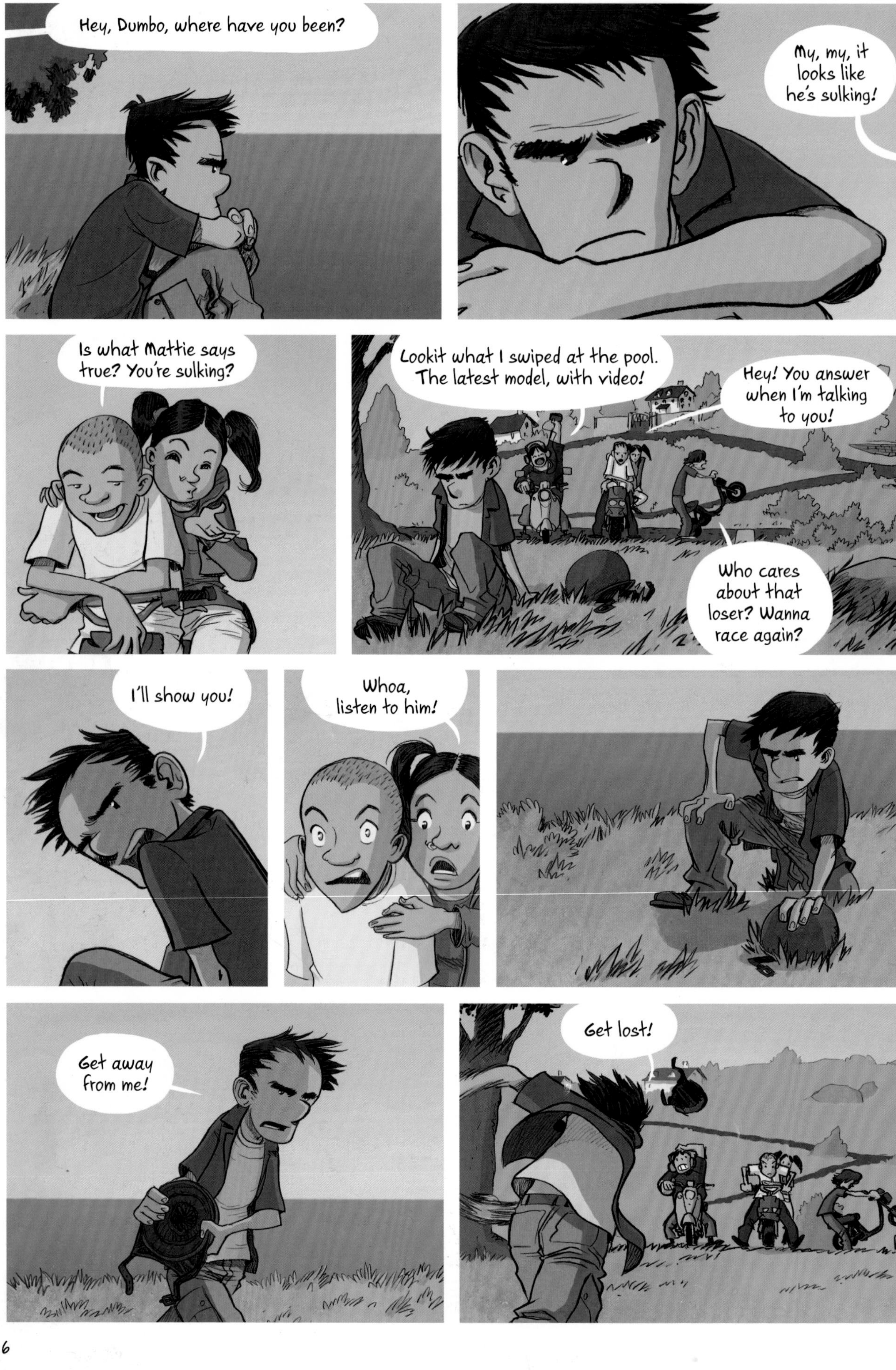

Hey, Dumbo, where have you been?
My, my, it looks like he's sulking!
Is what Mattie says true? You're sulking?
Lookit what I swiped at the pool. The latest model, with video!
Hey! You answer when I'm talking to you!
Who cares about that loser? Wanna race again?
I'll show you!
Whoa, listen to him!
Get away from me!
Get lost!

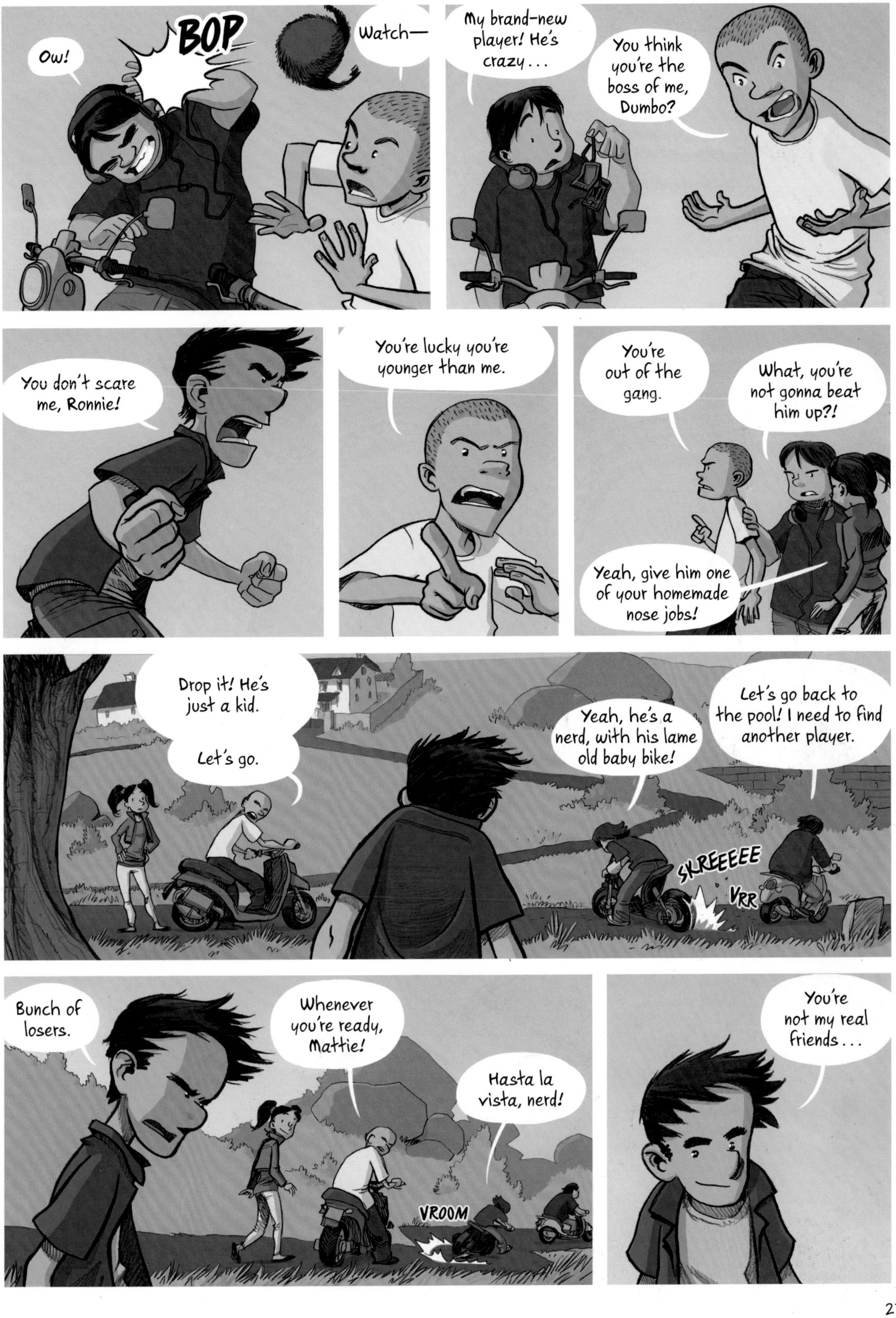
Ow!
BOP
Watch—
My brand-new player! He's crazy . . .
You think you're the boss of me, Dumbo?
You don't scare me, Ronnie!
You're lucky you're younger than me.
You're out of the gang.
What, you're not gonna beat him up?!
Yeah, give him one of your homemade nose jobs!
Drop it! He's just a kid.
Let's go.
Yeah, he's a nerd, with his lame old baby bike!
Let's go back to the pool! I need to find another player.
SKREEEEE
VRR
Bunch of losers.
Whenever you're ready, Mattie!
Hasta la vista, nerd!
VROOM
You're not my real friends . . .

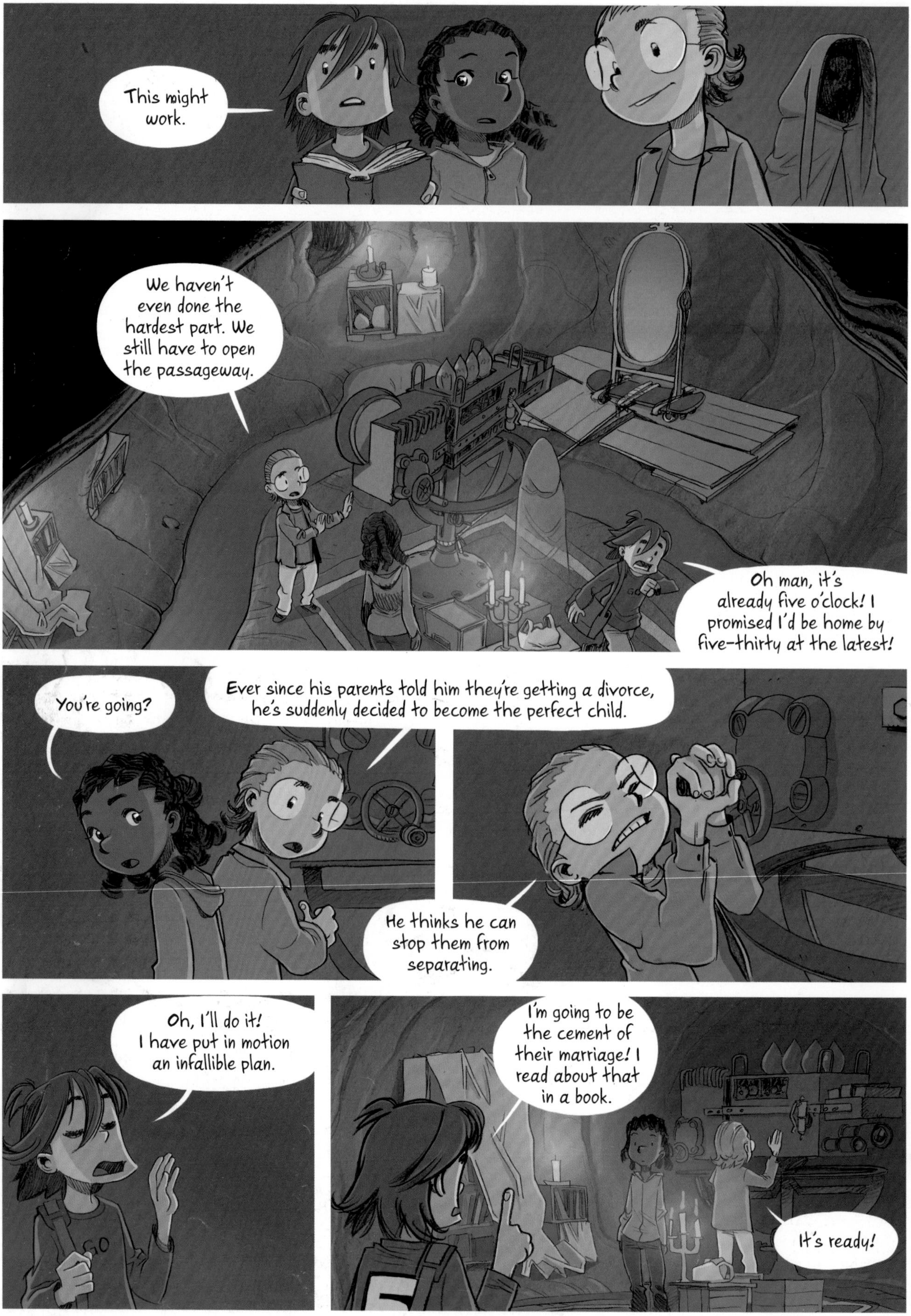
This might work.
We haven't even done the hardest part. We still have to open the passageway.
Oh man, it's already five o'clock! I promised I'd be home by five-thirty at the latest!
You're going?
Ever since his parents told him they're getting a divorce, he's suddenly decided to become the perfect child.
He thinks he can stop them from separating.
Oh, I'll do it! I have put in motion an infallible plan.
I'm going to be the cement of their marriage! I read about that in a book.
It's ready!

Noah, you get the mirror!

We're going to find this passageway!

All right, but fast, okay?

SHLAK

Rebecca, you must turn it as delicately as possible.

FLASH

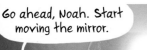
Go ahead, Noah. Start moving the mirror.

I think I know what to do. This reminds me of the time when my dad spent two days trying to set up a satellite dish to pick up some TV channels.

If he's anything like mine, he ended up calling a professional after getting all worked up about how the equipment supposedly wasn't made right.

Pretty much. But, it's a well-known fact, kids are often more gifted than their parents. Hehe...

I'm going to jam the machine's countdown mechanism. That'll keep me from having to turn it back on every two minutes.

Do you think that's wise?

As long as we stay on this side of the mirror, we're not taking many risks.

There.

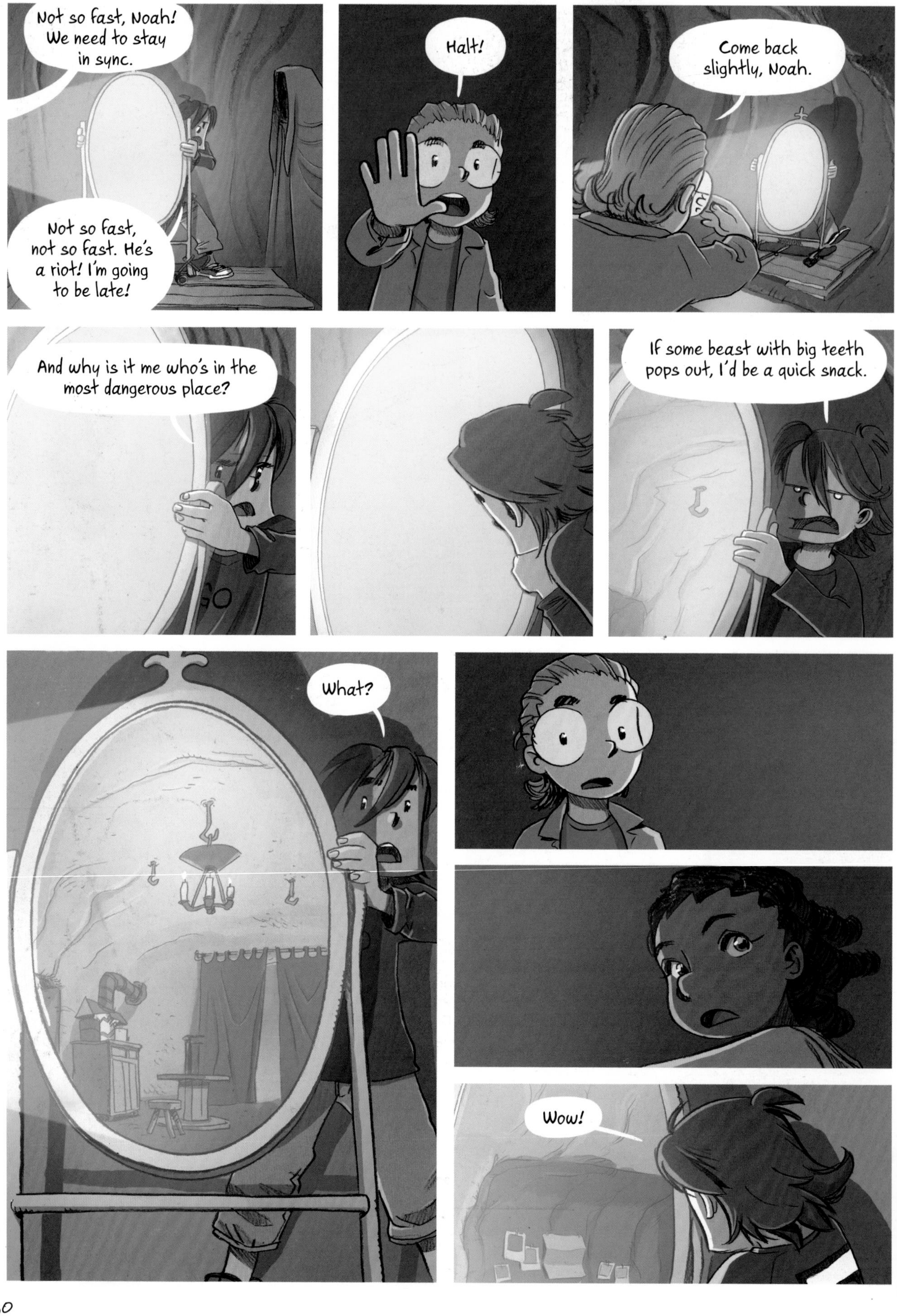
Not so fast, Noah! We need to stay in sync.
Not so fast, not so fast. He's a riot! I'm going to be late!
Halt!
Come back slightly, Noah.
And why is it me who's in the most dangerous place?
If some beast with big teeth pops out, I'd be a quick snack.
What?
Wow!

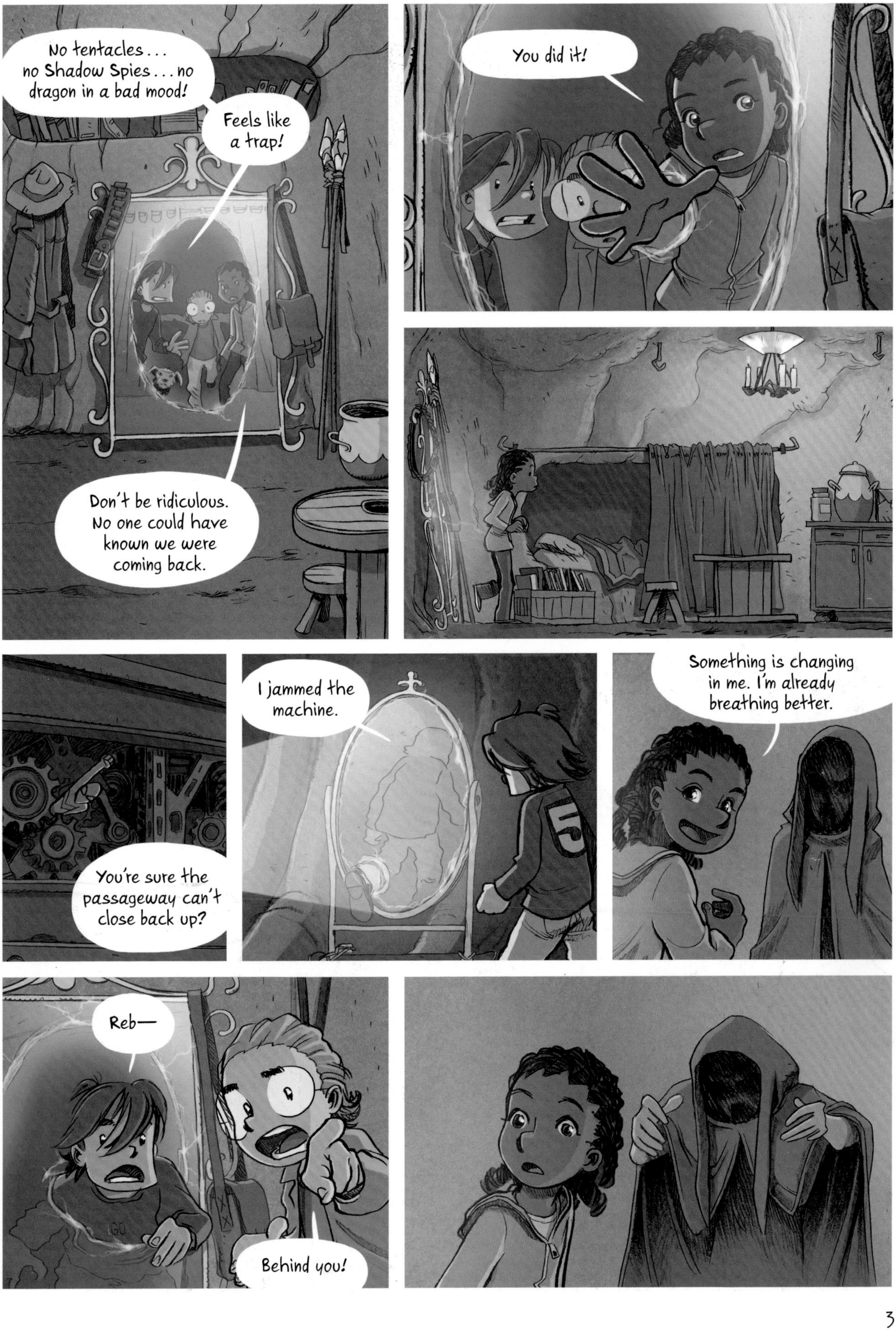
No tentacles . . . no Shadow Spies . . . no dragon in a bad mood!
Feels like a trap!
Don't be ridiculous. No one could have known we were coming back.
You did it!
I jammed the machine.
You're sure the passageway can't close back up?
Something is changing in me. I'm already breathing better.
Reb—
Behind you!

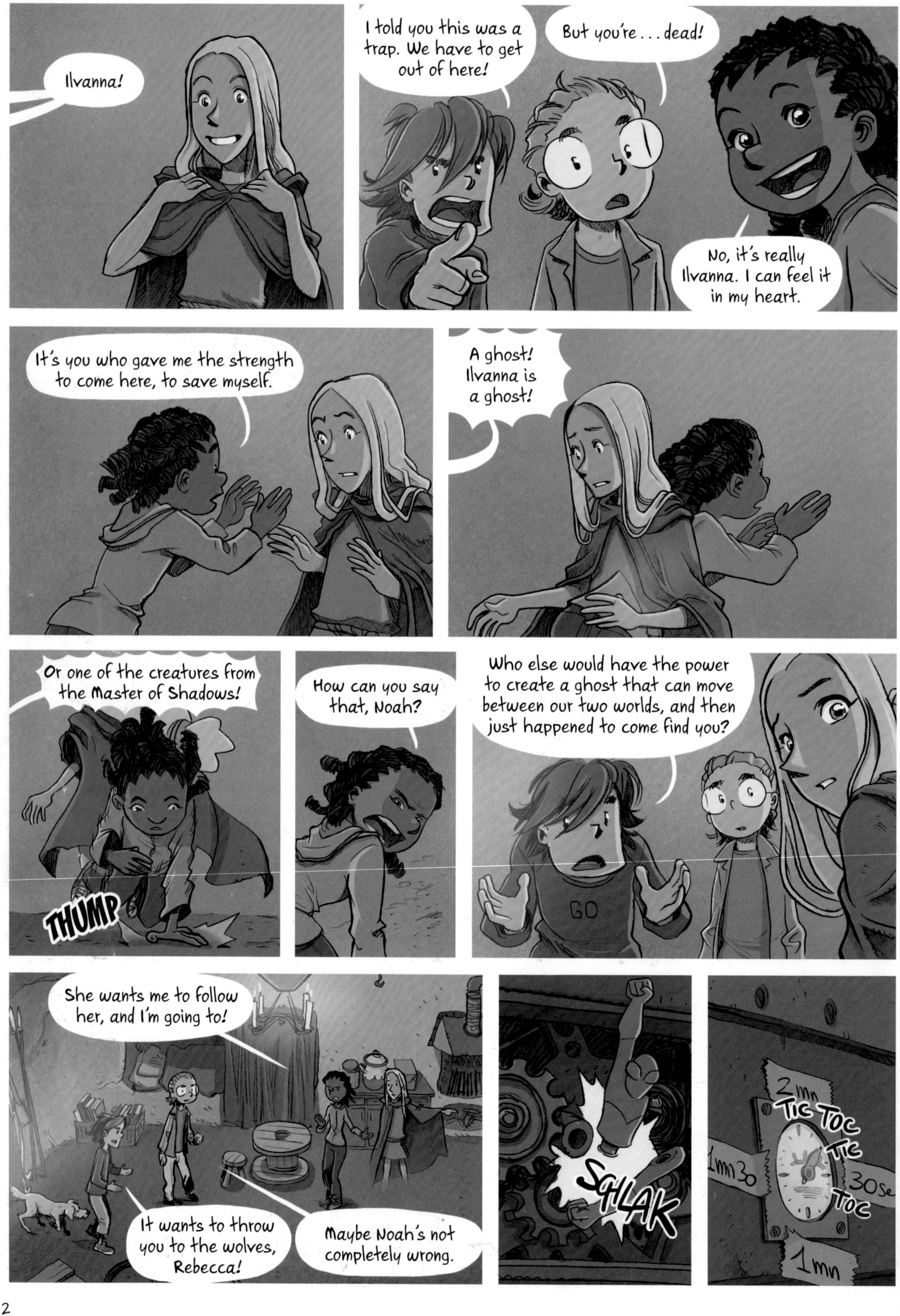
Ilvanna!
I told you this was a trap. We have to get out of here!
But you're . . . dead!
No, it's really Ilvanna. I can feel it in my heart.
It's you who gave me the strength to come here, to save myself.
A ghost! Ilvanna is a ghost!
Or one of the creatures from the Master of Shadows!
THUMP
How can you say that, Noah?
Who else would have the power to create a ghost that can move between our two worlds, and then just happened to come find you?
GO
She wants me to follow her, and I'm going to!
It wants to throw you to the wolves, Rebecca!
Maybe Noah's not completely wrong.
SCHLAK
2mn
TIC TOC
TIC
1mn30
30se
TOC
1mn

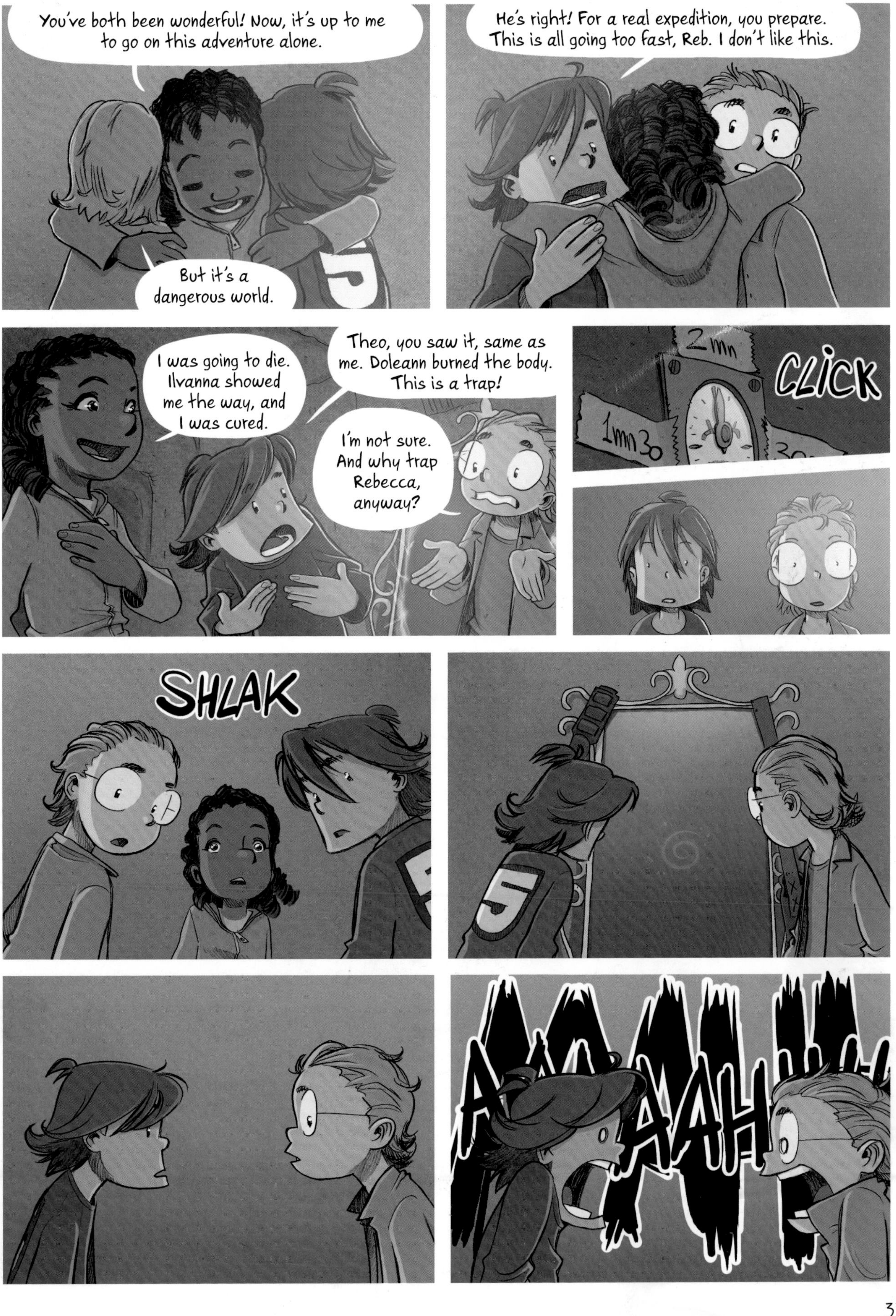
You've both been wonderful! Now, it's up to me to go on this adventure alone.
But it's a dangerous world.
He's right! For a real expedition, you prepare. This is all going too fast, Reb. I don't like this.
I was going to die. Ilvanna showed me the way, and I was cured.
Theo, you saw it, same as me. Doleann burned the body. This is a trap!
I'm not sure. And why trap Rebecca, anyway?
2mn
1mn30
CLICK
SHLAK
AAAAAH

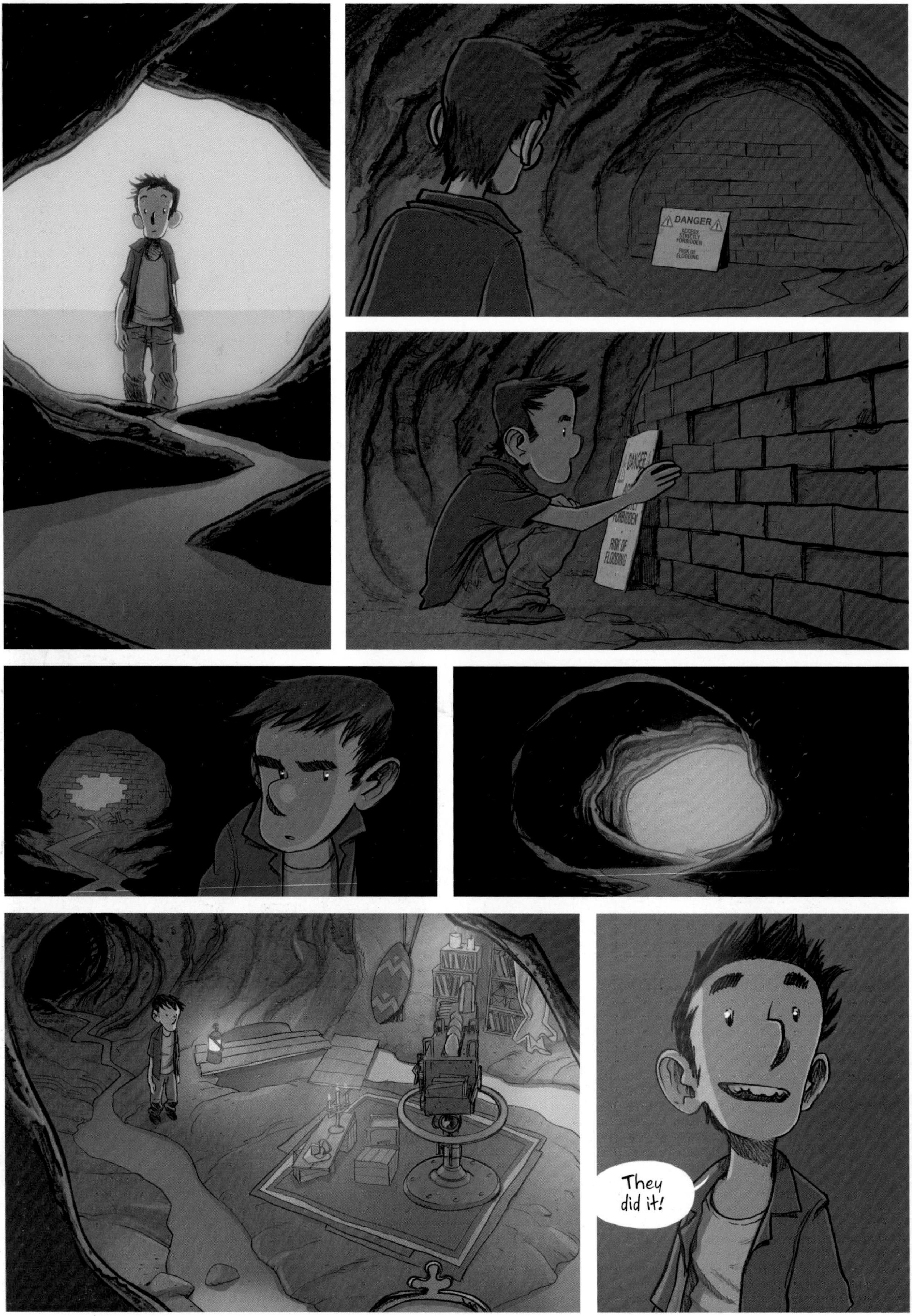
DANGER
ACCESS STRICTLY FORBIDDEN
RISK OF FLOODING
They did it!

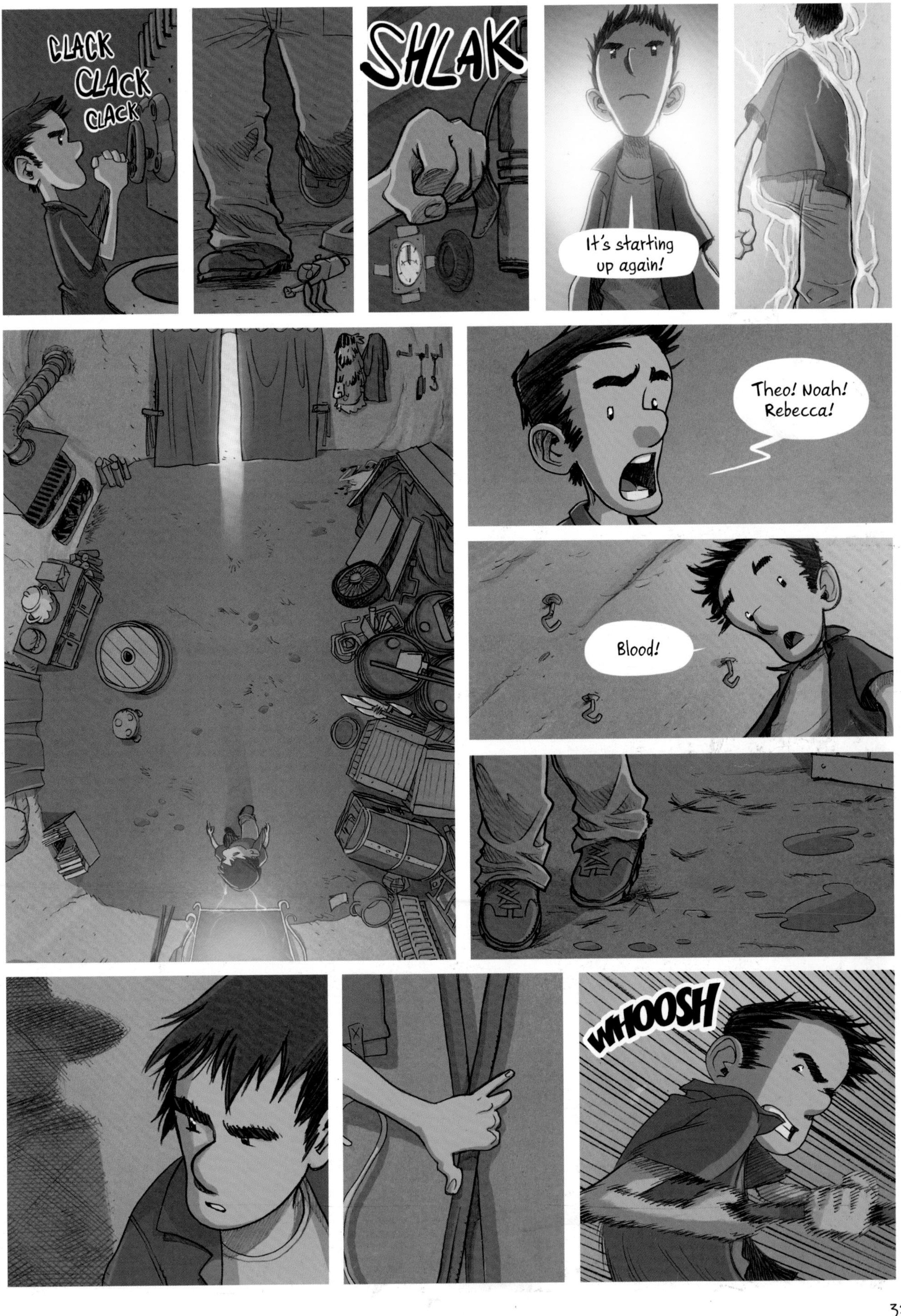
CLACK
CLACK
CLACK
SHLAK
It's starting up again!
Theo! Noah! Rebecca!
Blood!
WHOOSH

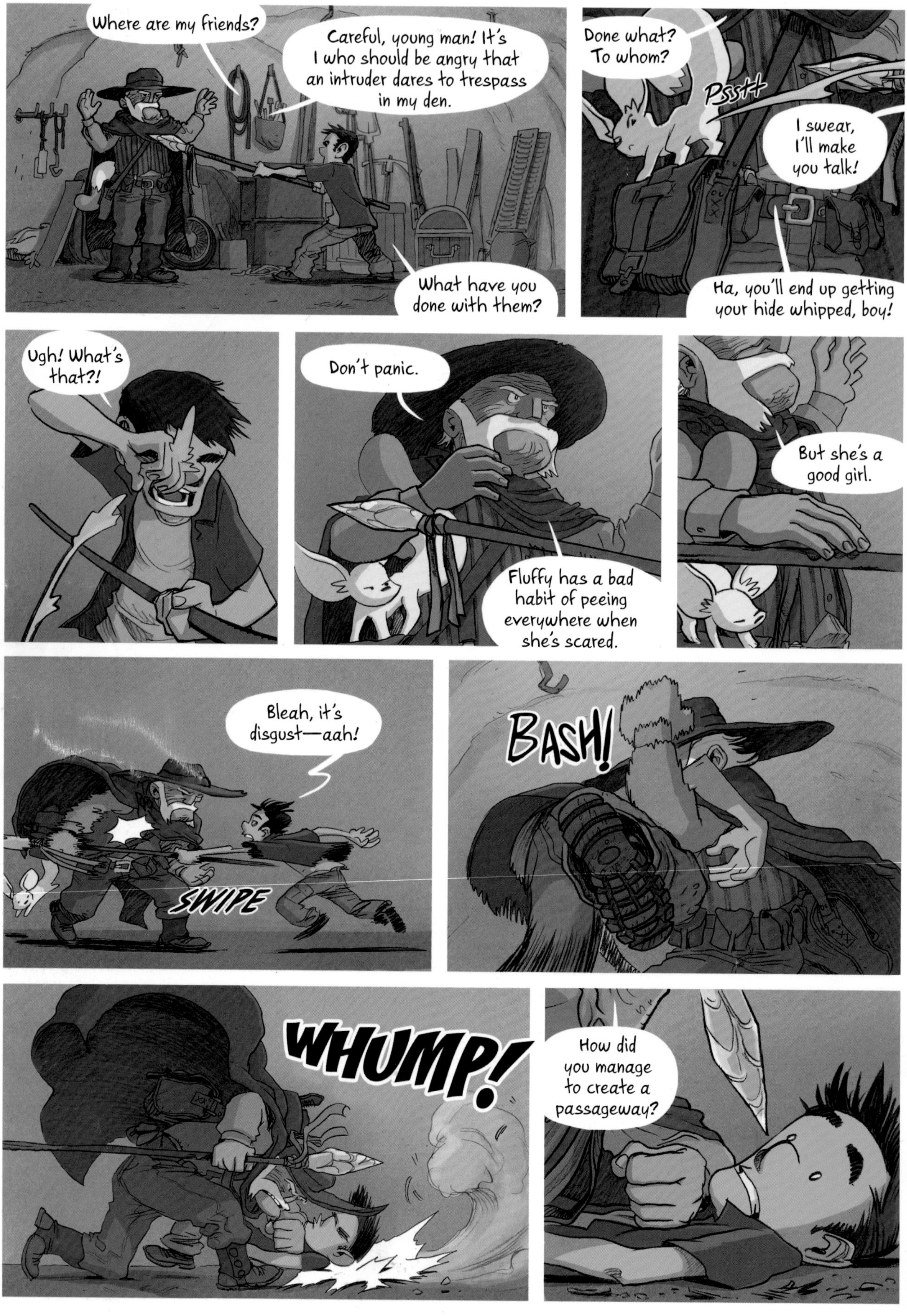
Where are my friends?
Careful, young man! It's I who should be angry that an intruder dares to trespass in my den.
What have you done with them?
Done what? To whom?
Psstt
I swear, I'll make you talk!
Ha, you'll end up getting your hide whipped, boy!
Ugh! What's that?!
Don't panic.
Fluffy has a bad habit of peeing everywhere when she's scared.
But she's a good girl.
Bleah, it's disgust—aah!
SWIPE
BASH!
WHUMP!
How did you manage to create a passageway?

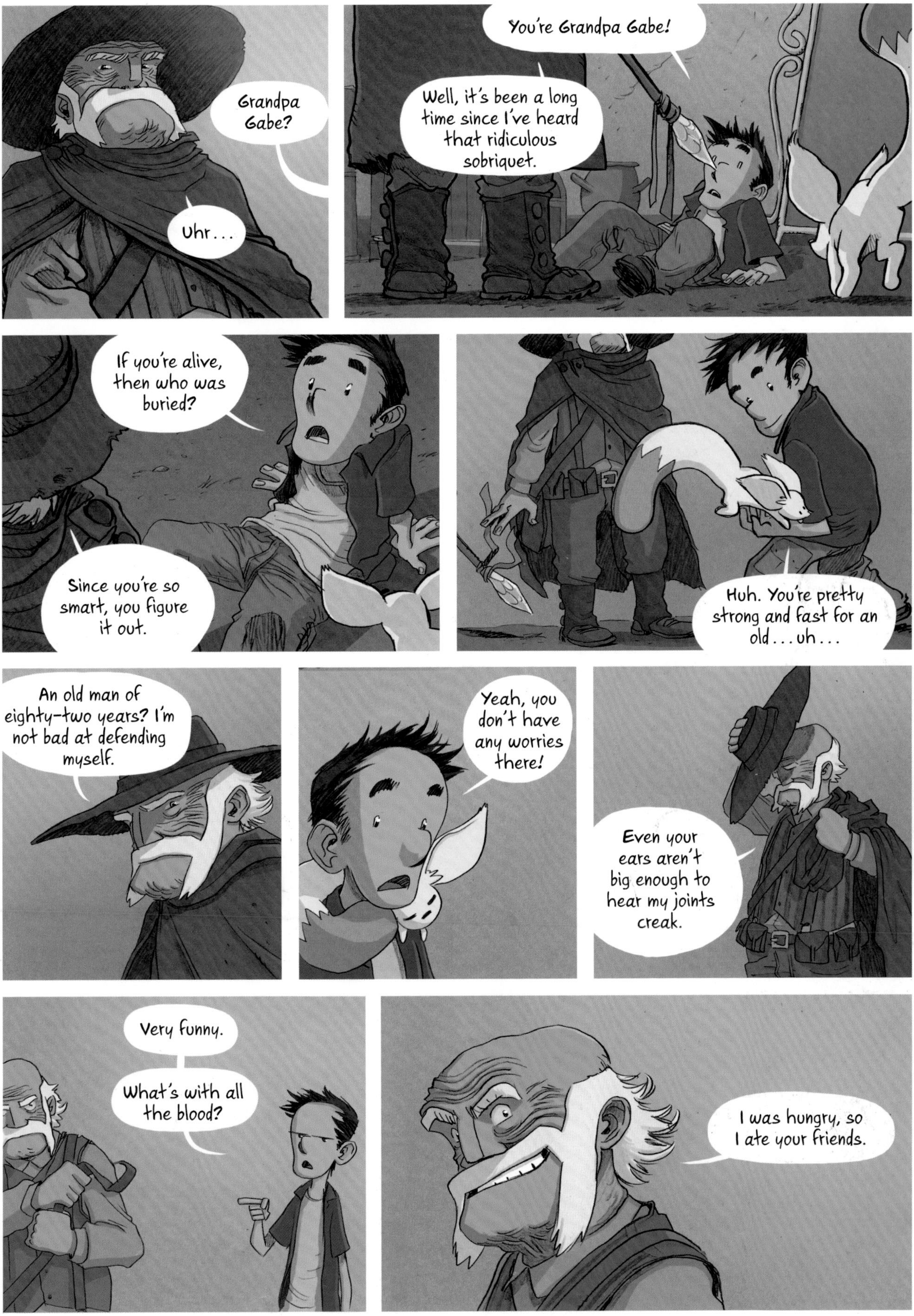
Grandpa Gabe?
Uhr...
You're Grandpa Gabe!
Well, it's been a long time since I've heard that ridiculous sobriquet.
If you're alive, then who was buried?
Since you're so smart, you figure it out.
Huh. You're pretty strong and fast for an old...uh...
An old man of eighty-two years? I'm not bad at defending myself.
Yeah, you don't have any worries there!
Even your ears aren't big enough to hear my joints creak.
Very funny.
What's with all the blood?
I was hungry, so I ate your friends.

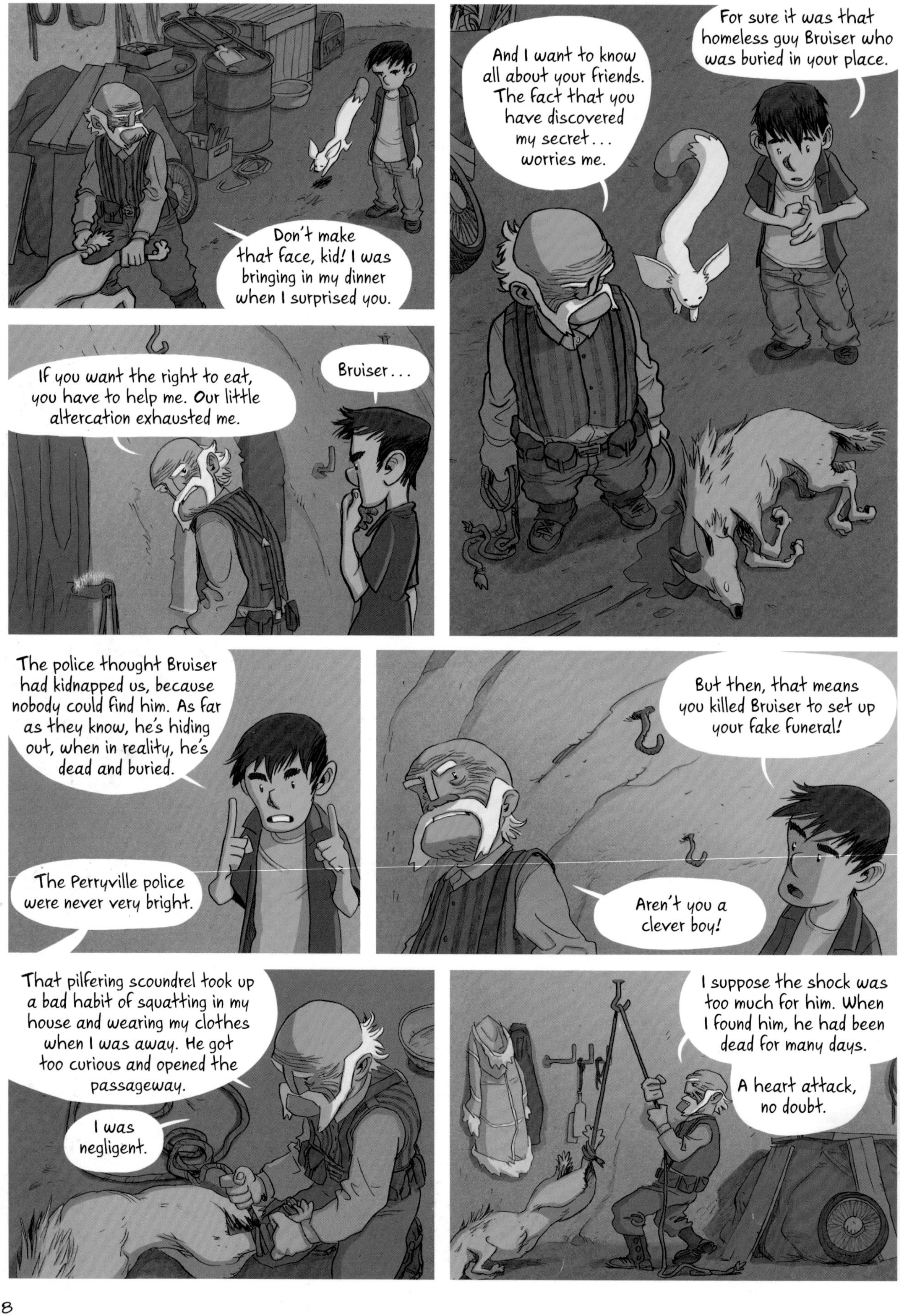
Don't make that face, kid! I was bringing in my dinner when I surprised you.
If you want the right to eat, you have to help me. Our little altercation exhausted me.
Bruiser...
And I want to know all about your friends. The fact that you have discovered my secret... worries me.
For sure it was that homeless guy Bruiser who was buried in your place.
The police thought Bruiser had kidnapped us, because nobody could find him. As far as they know, he's hiding out, when in reality, he's dead and buried.
The Perryville police were never very bright.
But then, that means you killed Bruiser to set up your fake funeral!
Aren't you a clever boy!
That pilfering scoundrel took up a bad habit of squatting in my house and wearing my clothes when I was away. He got too curious and opened the passageway.
I was negligent.
I suppose the shock was too much for him. When I found him, he had been dead for many days.
A heart attack, no doubt.

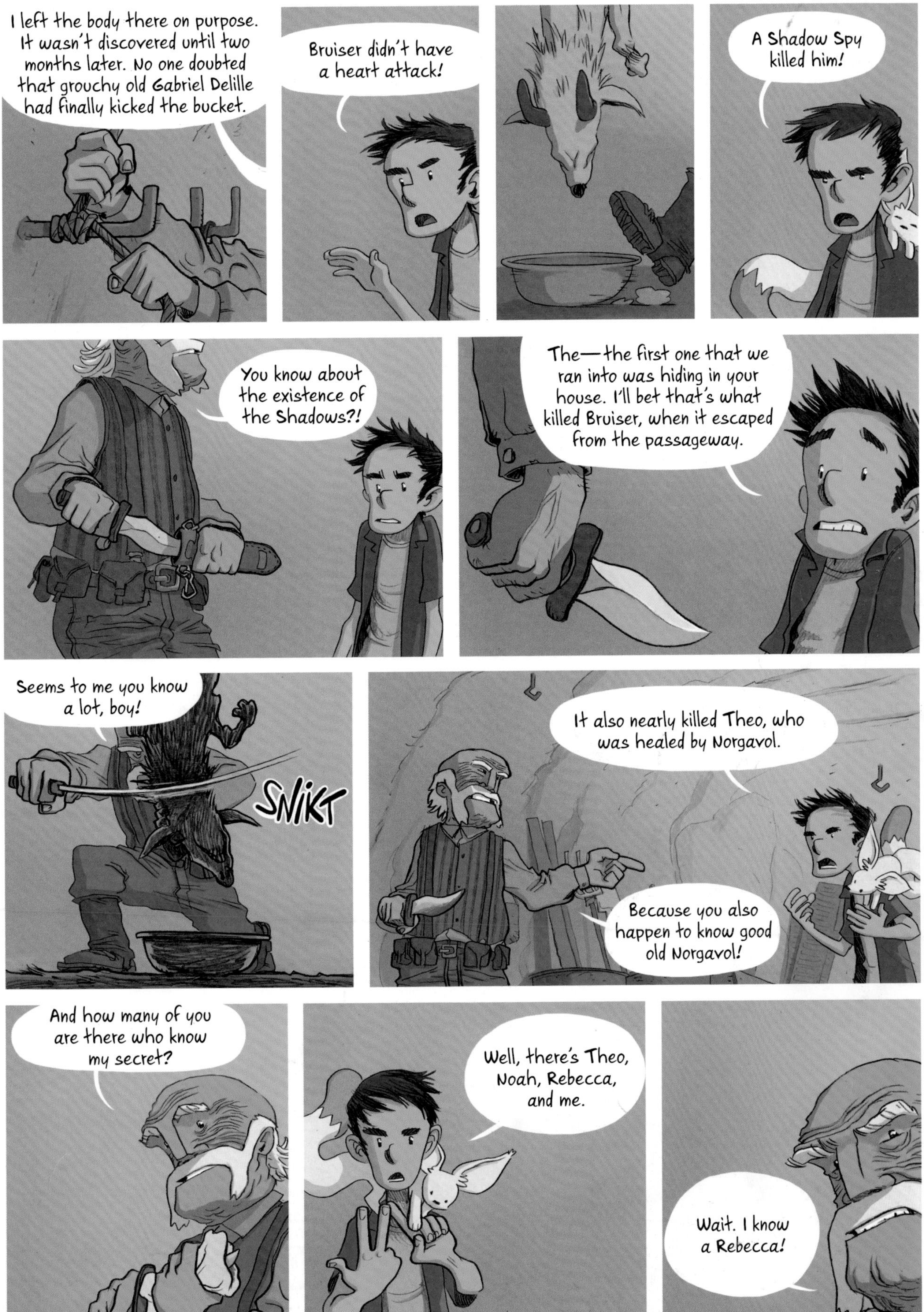
I left the body there on purpose. It wasn't discovered until two months later. No one doubted that grouchy old Gabriel Delille had finally kicked the bucket.
Bruiser didn't have a heart attack!
A Shadow Spy killed him!
You know about the existence of the Shadows?!
The—the first one that we ran into was hiding in your house. I'll bet that's what killed Bruiser, when it escaped from the passageway.
Seems to me you know a lot, boy!
SNIKT
It also nearly killed Theo, who was healed by Norgavol.
Because you also happen to know good old Norgavol!
And how many of you are there who know my secret?
Well, there's Theo, Noah, Rebecca, and me.
Wait. I know a Rebecca!

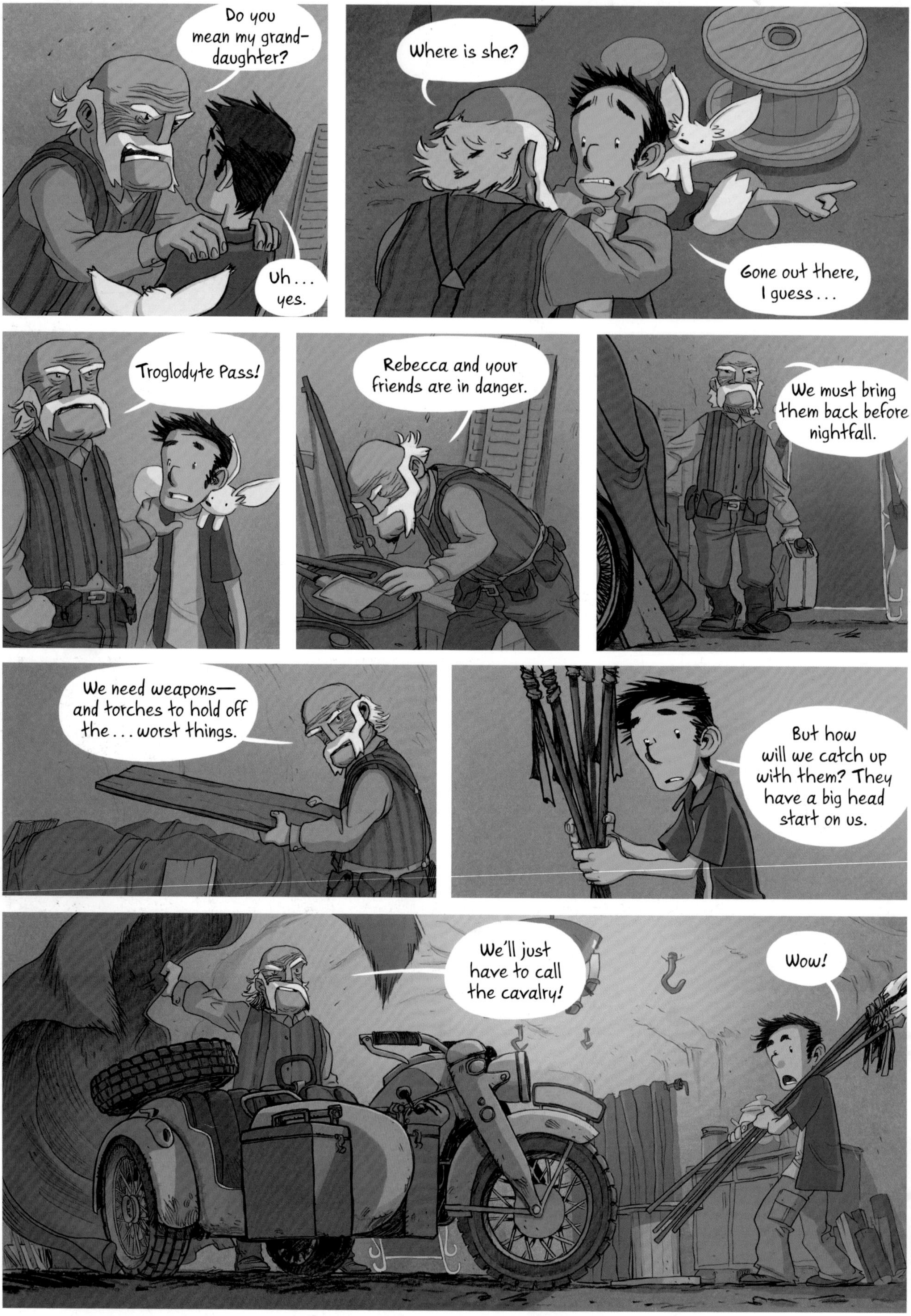

Do you mean my grand-daughter?
Uh... yes.
Where is she?
Gone out there, I guess...
Troglodyte Pass!
Rebecca and your friends are in danger.
We must bring them back before nightfall.
We need weapons—and torches to hold off the... worst things.
But how will we catch up with them? They have a big head start on us.
We'll just have to call the cavalry!
Wow!

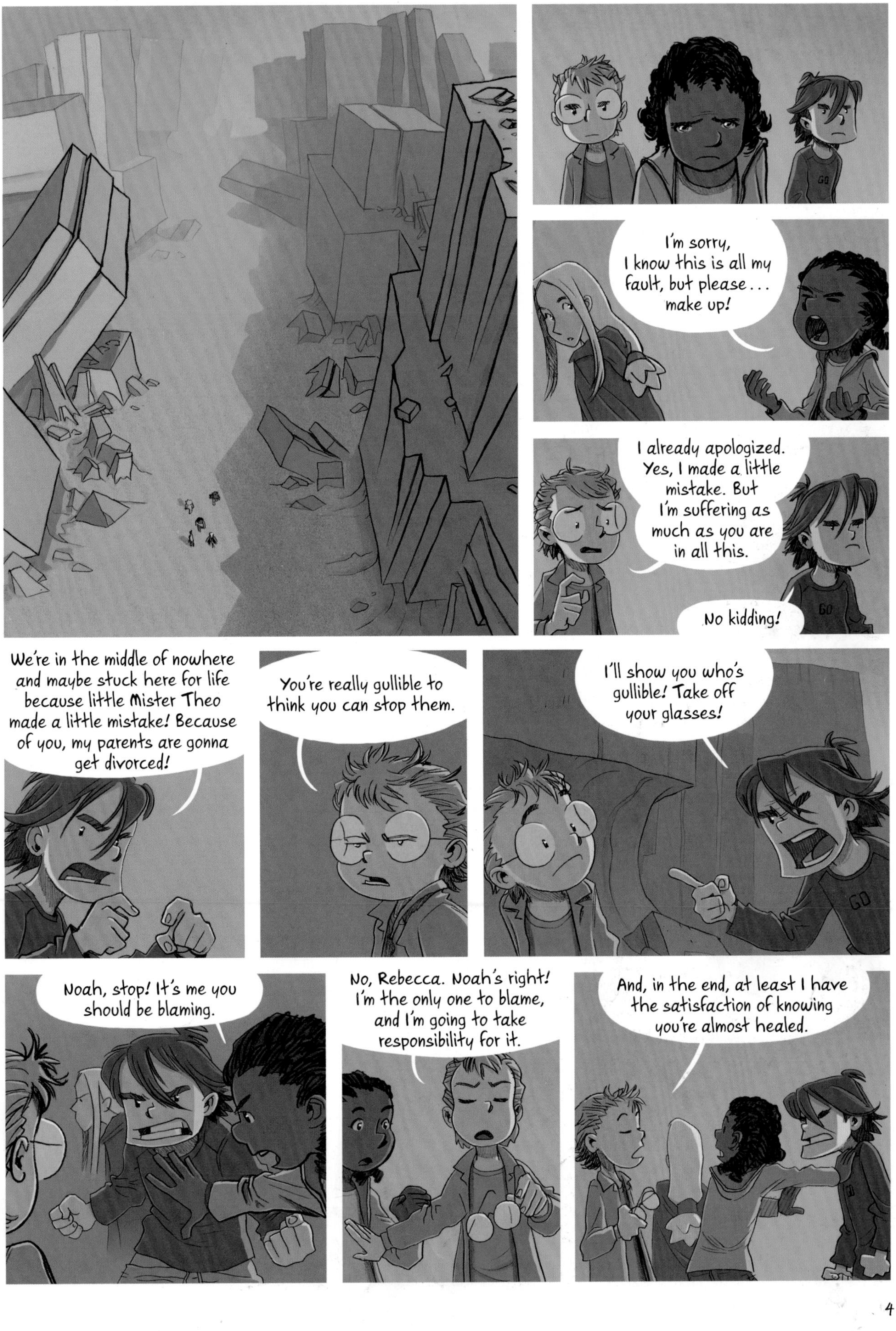
I'm sorry, I know this is all my fault, but please... make up!
I already apologized. Yes, I made a little mistake. But I'm suffering as much as you are in all this.
No kidding!
We're in the middle of nowhere and maybe stuck here for life because little Mister Theo made a little mistake! Because of you, my parents are gonna get divorced!
You're really gullible to think you can stop them.
I'll show you who's gullible! Take off your glasses!
Noah, stop! It's me you should be blaming.
No, Rebecca. Noah's right! I'm the only one to blame, and I'm going to take responsibility for it.
And, in the end, at least I have the satisfaction of knowing you're almost healed.

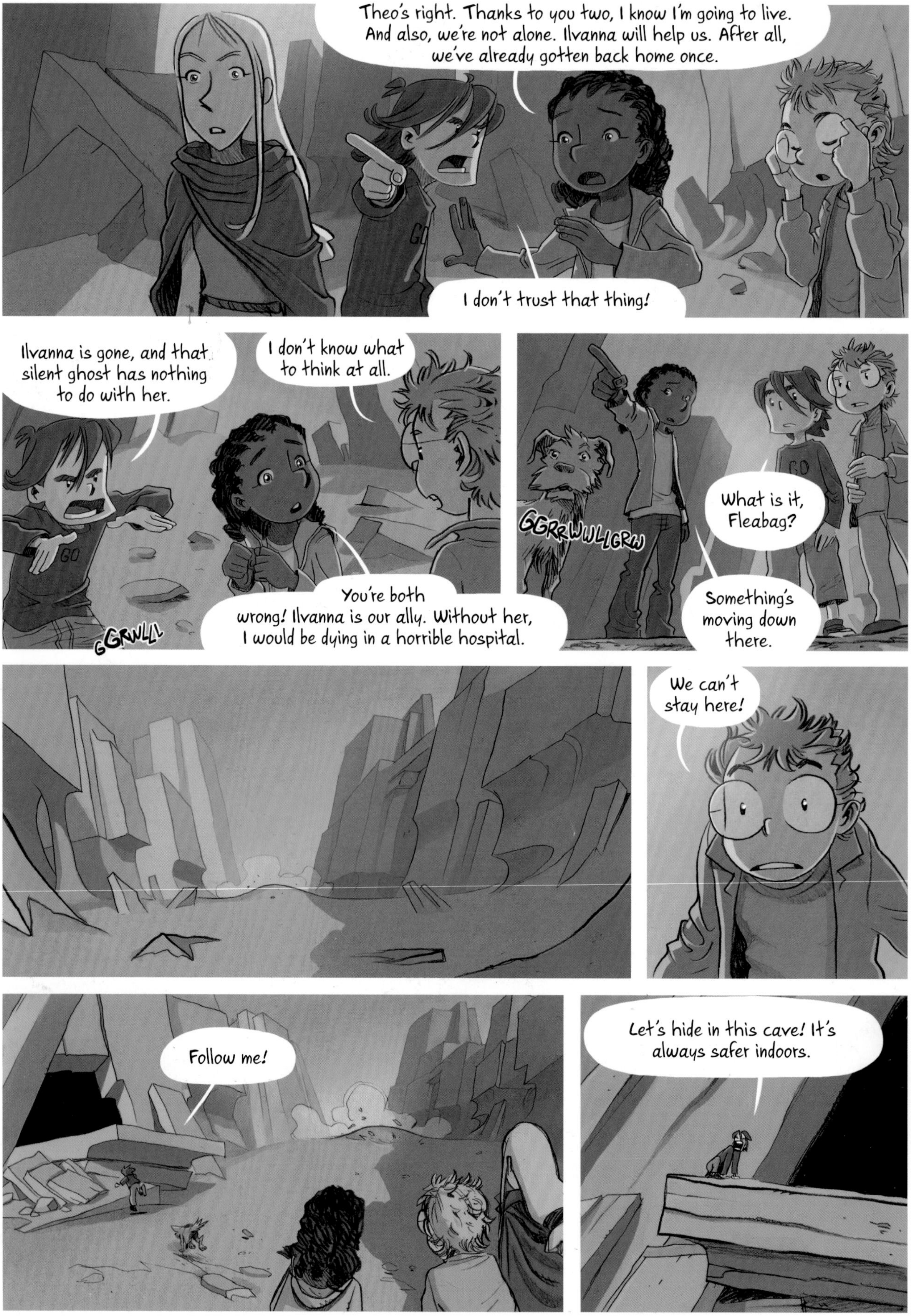
Theo's right. Thanks to you two, I know I'm going to live. And also, we're not alone. Ilvanna will help us. After all, we've already gotten back home once.
I don't trust that thing!
Ilvanna is gone, and that silent ghost has nothing to do with her.
I don't know what to think at all.
You're both wrong! Ilvanna is our ally. Without her, I would be dying in a horrible hospital.
GGRWLLL
GGRRWWLLGRW
What is it, Fleabag?
Something's moving down there.
We can't stay here!
Follow me!
Let's hide in this cave! It's always safer indoors.

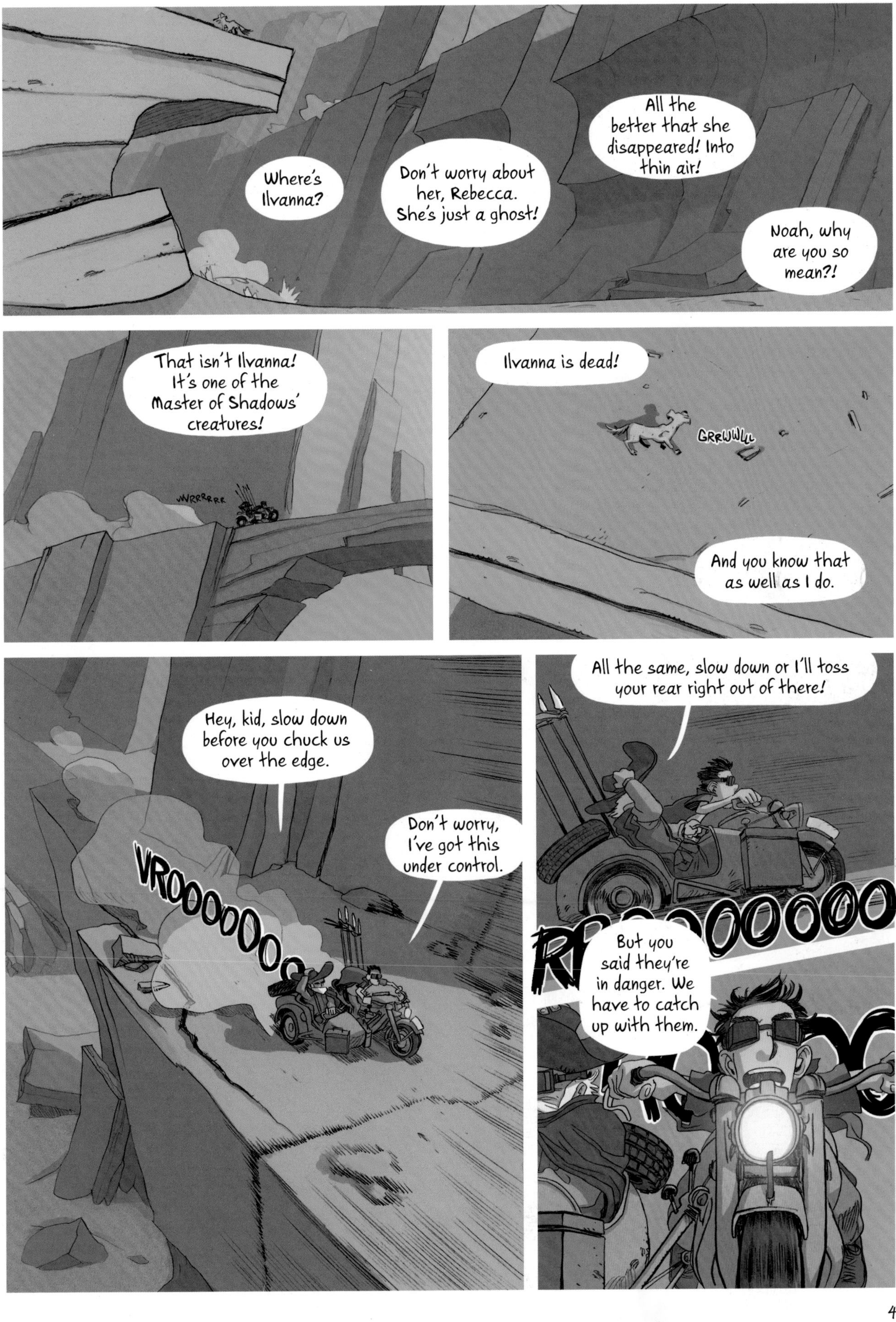
Where's Ilvanna?
Don't worry about her, Rebecca. She's just a ghost!
All the better that she disappeared! Into thin air!
Noah, why are you so mean?!
That isn't Ilvanna! It's one of the Master of Shadows' creatures!
Ilvanna is dead!
And you know that as well as I do.
Hey, kid, slow down before you chuck us over the edge.
Don't worry, I've got this under control.
All the same, slow down or I'll toss your rear right out of there!
But you said they're in danger. We have to catch up with them.

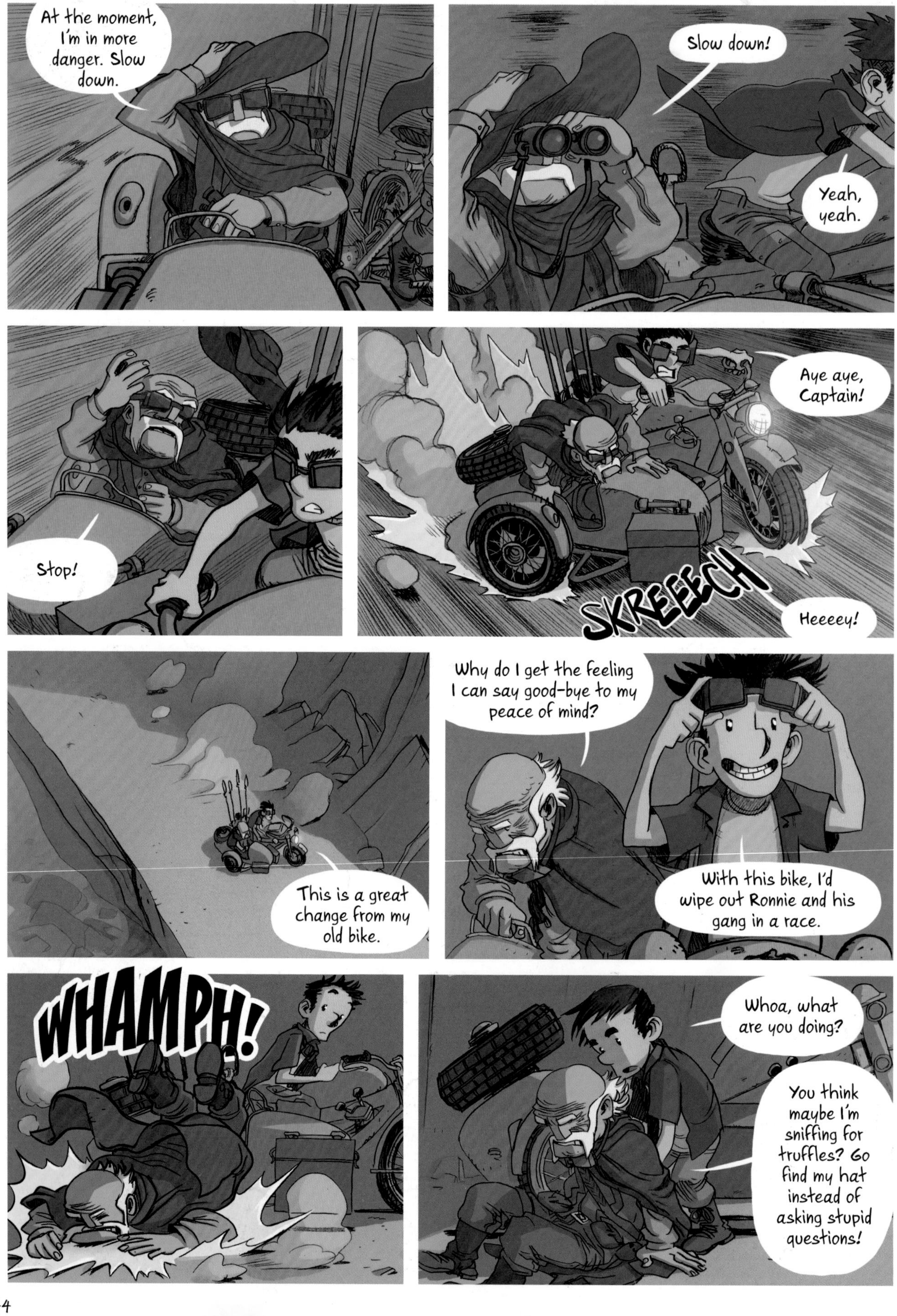
At the moment, I'm in more danger. Slow down.
Slow down!
Yeah, yeah.
Stop!
Aye aye, Captain!
SKREEECH
Heeeey!
This is a great change from my old bike.
Why do I get the feeling I can say good-bye to my peace of mind?
With this bike, I'd wipe out Ronnie and his gang in a race.
WHAMPH!
Whoa, what are you doing?
You think maybe I'm sniffing for truffles? Go find my hat instead of asking stupid questions!

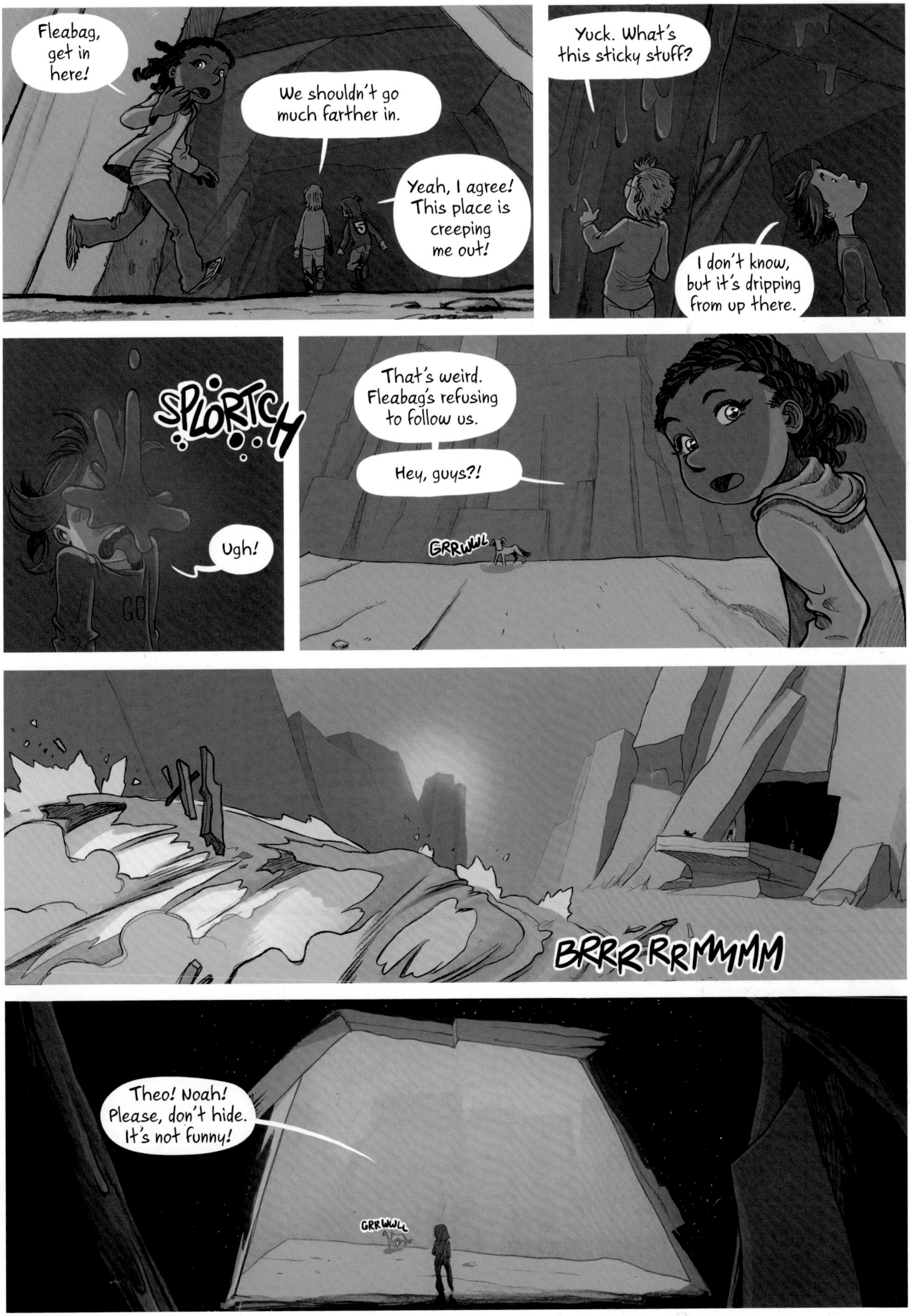
Fleabag, get in here!
We shouldn't go much farther in.
Yeah, I agree! This place is creeping me out!
Yuck. What's this sticky stuff?
I don't know, but it's dripping from up there.
SPLORTCH
Ugh!
That's weird. Fleabag's refusing to follow us.
Hey, guys?!
GRRWWL
BRRRRRMMMM
Theo! Noah! Please, don't hide. It's not funny!
GRRWWLL

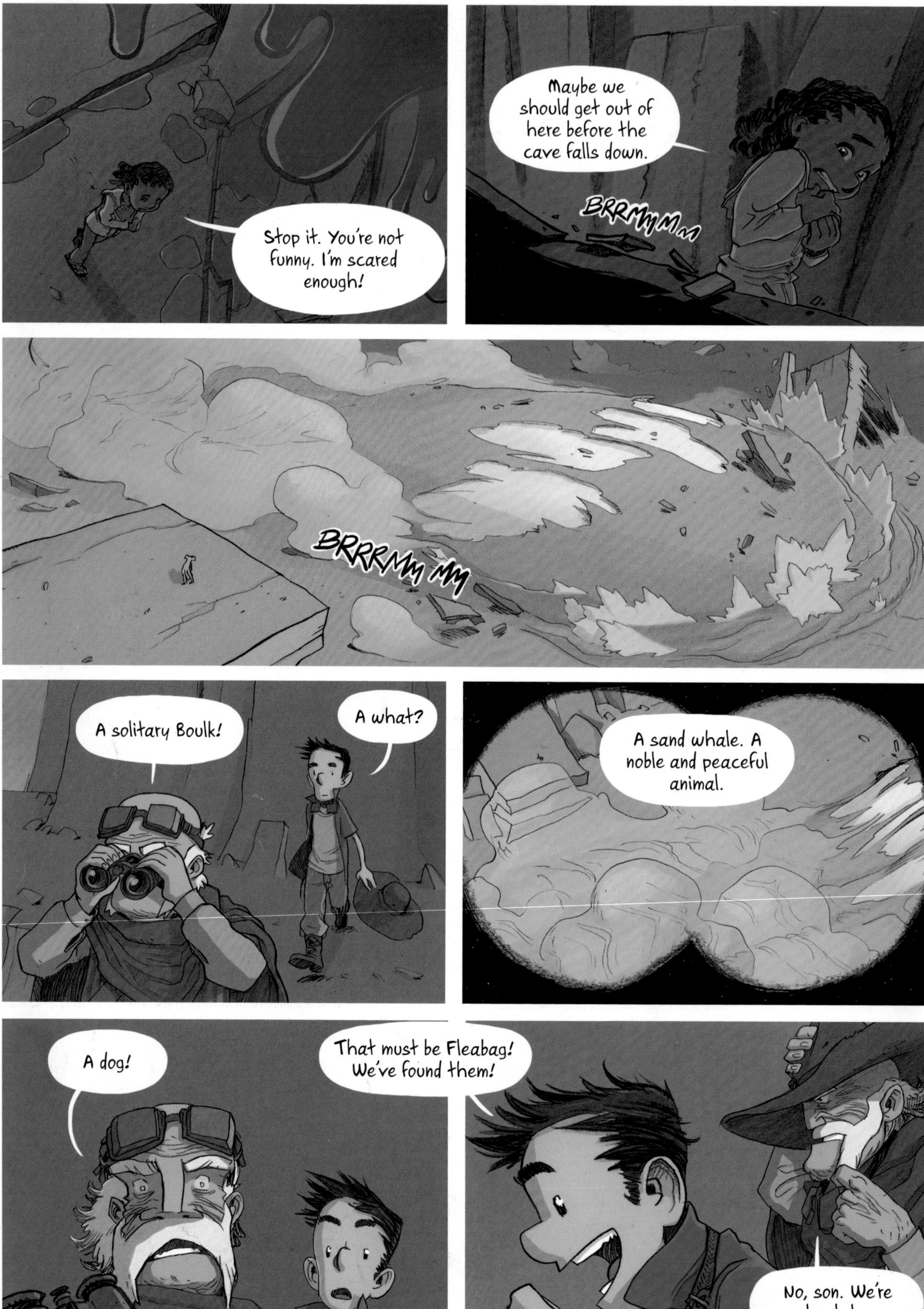

Stop it. You're not funny. I'm scared enough!
Maybe we should get out of here before the cave falls down.
BRRMMMMM
BRRRMM MM
A solitary Boulk!
A what?
A sand whale. A noble and peaceful animal.
A dog!
That must be Fleabag! We've found them!
No, son. We're too late.

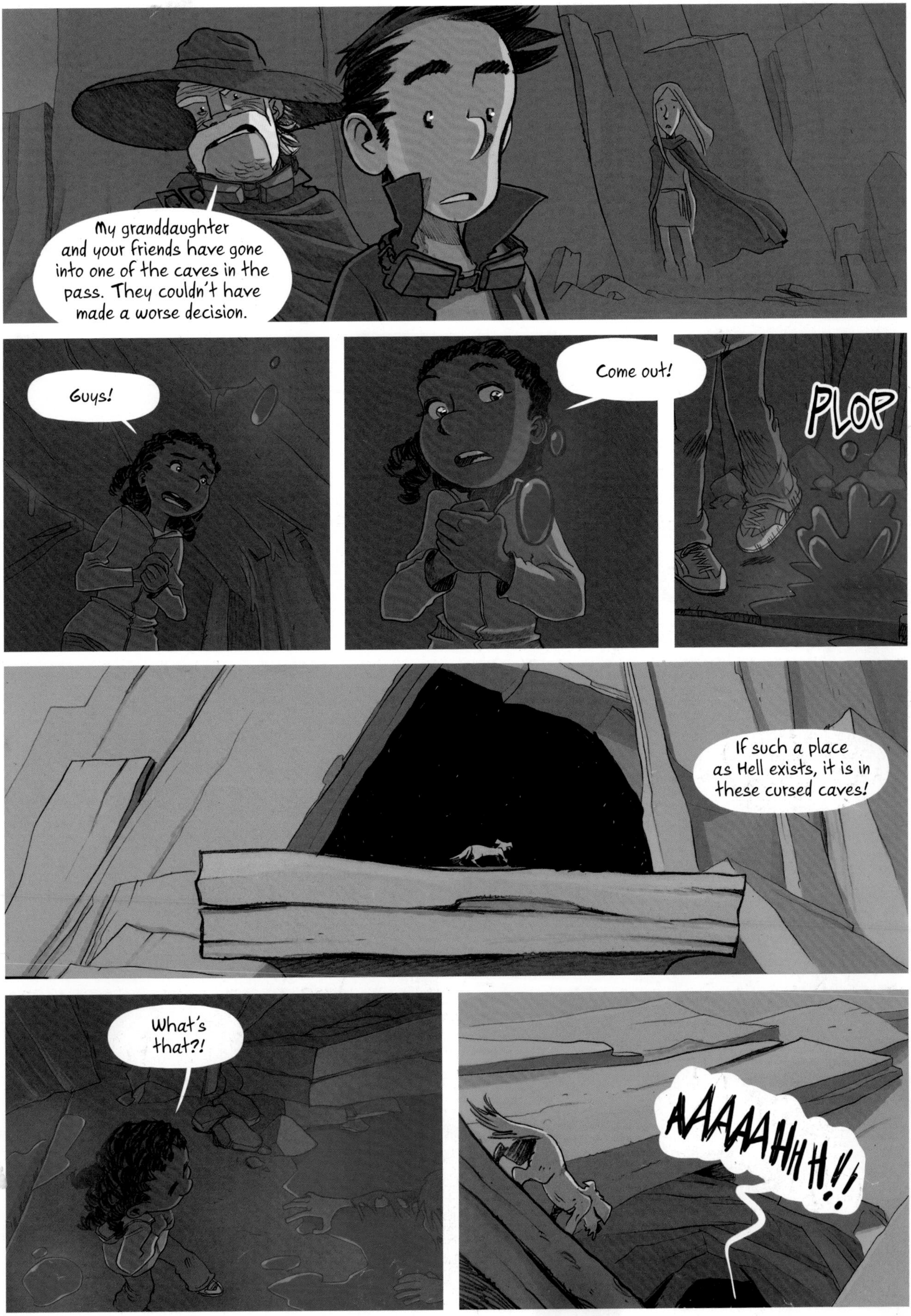
My granddaughter and your friends have gone into one of the caves in the pass. They couldn't have made a worse decision.
Guys!
Come out!
PLOP
If such a place as Hell exists, it is in these cursed caves!
What's that?!
AAAAAHHH!!

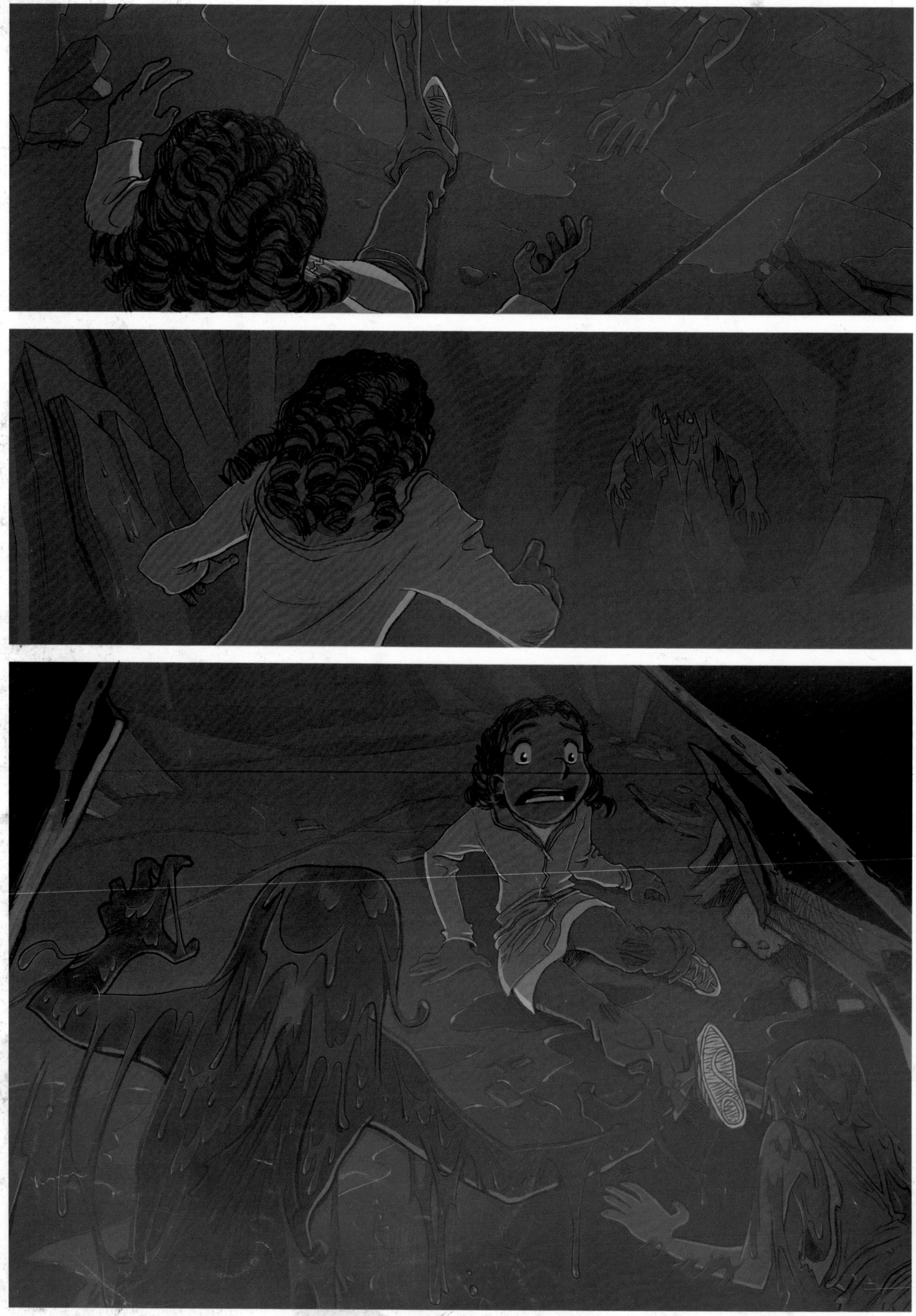

To be continued...

Art by Bannister
Story by Nykko
Colors by Jaffré
Translation by Carol Klio Burrell

First American edition published in 2010 by Graphic Universe™.
Published by arrangement with Mediatoon Licensing—France.

Graphic Universe™
A division of Lerner Publishing Group, Inc.
241 First Avenue North
Minneapolis, MN 55401 U.S.A.

Website address: www.lernerbooks.com

Library of Congress Cataloging-in-Publication Data

Bannister.
Book four: The calling / art by Bannister ;
story by Nykko. — 1st American ed.
p.   cm. — (ElseWhere chronicles ; bk. 4)
Summary: Rebecca, convinced that she will die if she does not
return to the other world, enlists the help of Theo and Noah to open
a new passageway, but once on the other side they fall into danger
and Max, unaware of the peril, follows.
ISBN: 978-0-7613-6068-1 (lib. bdg. : alk. paper)
1. Graphic novels. [1. Graphic novels. 2. Horror stories.] I. Nykko.
II. Title.
PZ7.7.B34Cal 2010
741.5'973—dc22   2009037643

Manufactured in the United States of America
2 - BP - 6/1/10

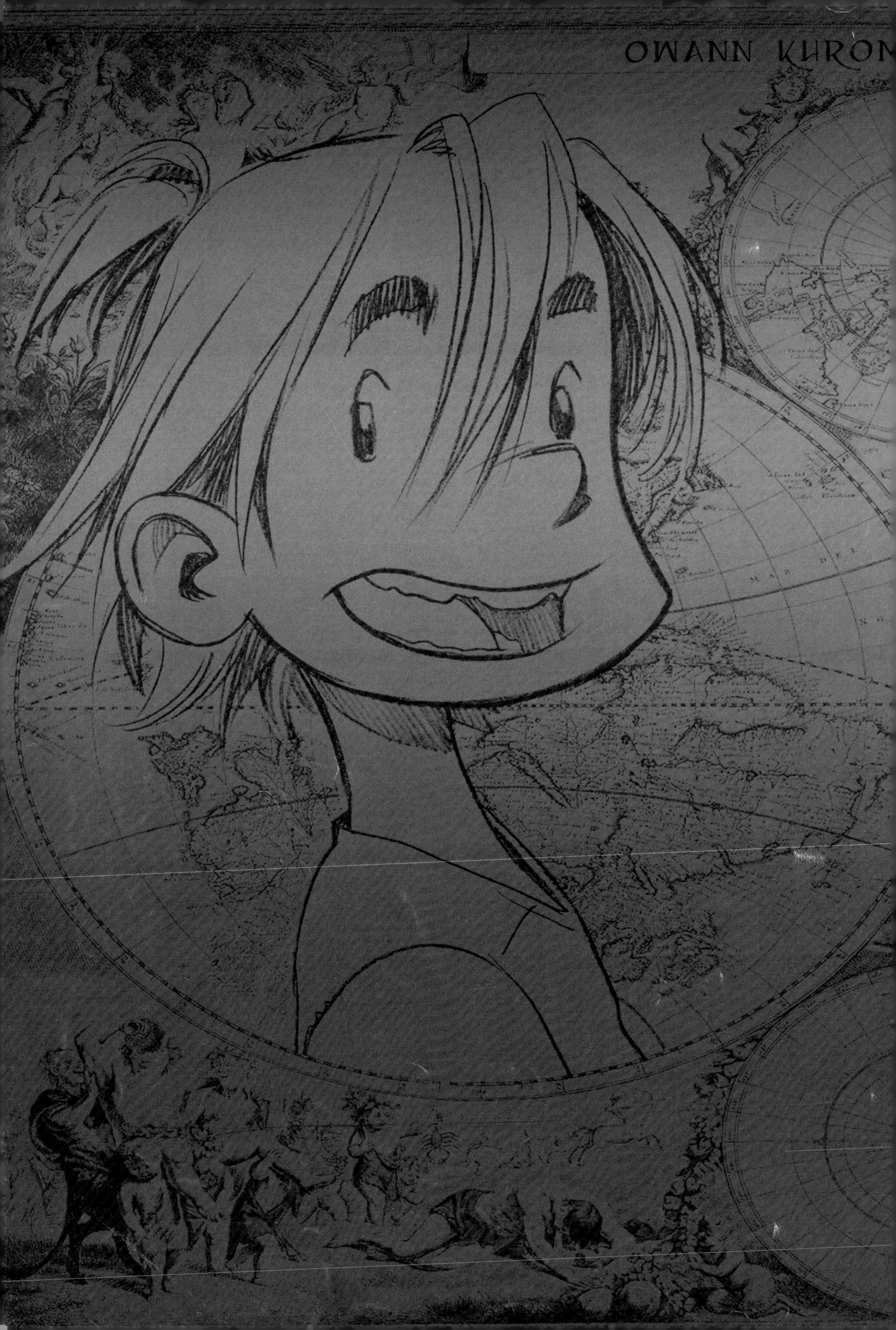
OWANN KUHON

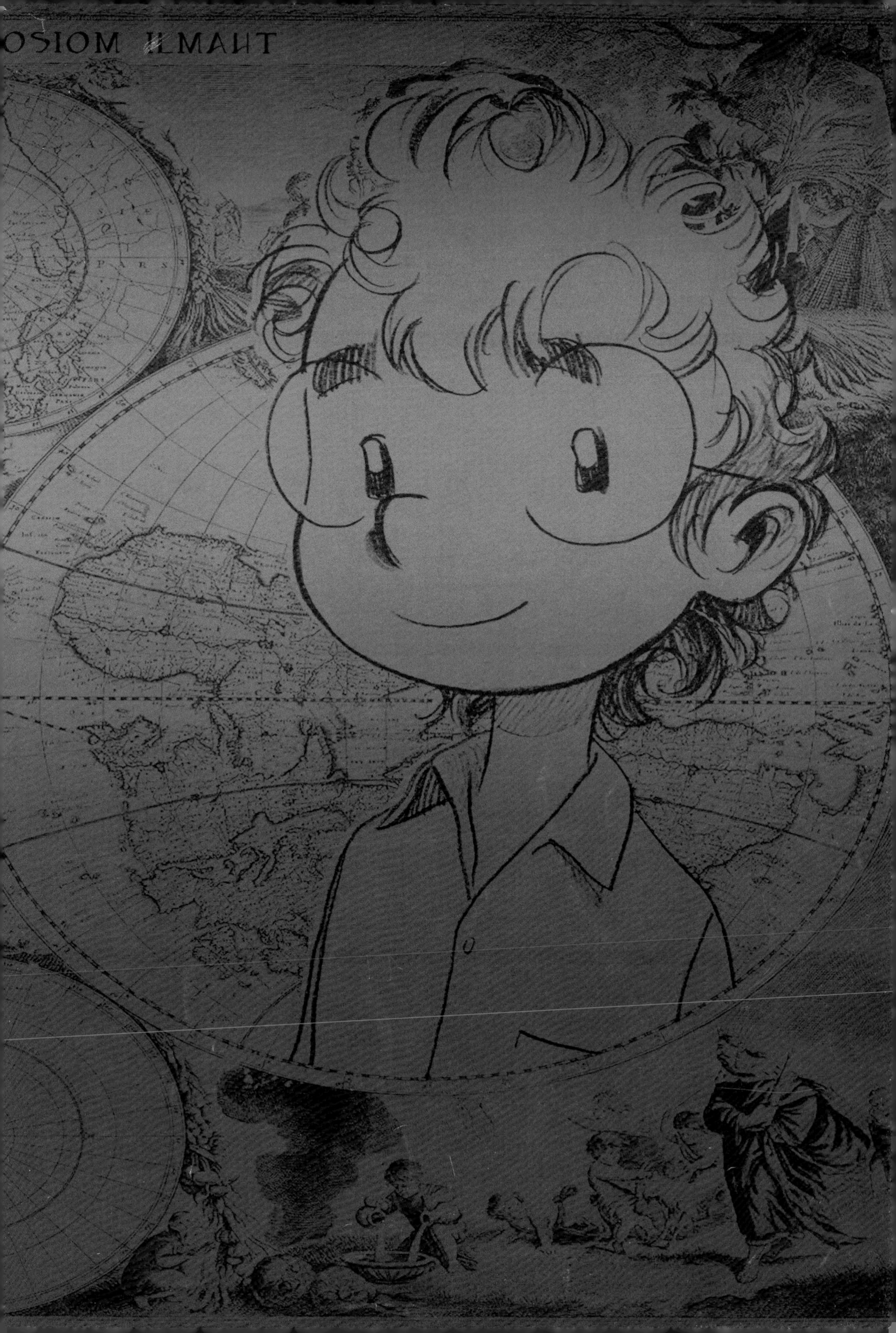